"What do you think? Does this say Montana cowgirl or is it too Pacific Northwest lumberjack?"

Hank didn't know what he'd expected to see when Gemma pulled back that curtain. After all, at their first meeting, she'd been wearing less material than it took to make a handkerchief. He knew how gorgeous she was. Sexy, sophisticated, big-city chic. Everything about that woman had exuded *look but don't touch.* But this...

Skintight indigo denim hugged her long legs, skimming over every curve in a way that had his palms tingling to do the same. As his hungry gaze moved upward, he took in the sleeveless blouse she'd chosen. Not the checked one she'd held up earlier, but a red bandanna print that showed off the toned muscles and smooth skin of her arms.

This was girl next door...all grown up.

And all the reasons why Hank had told himself to keep his distance—the differences in their lives, in their locations, his reluctance to risk his heart in any kind of relationship—seemed to have been brushed aside with one magical swipe of a dressing-room curtain.

"It looks just like..."

"Like what?" he asked when her voice trailed off.

"Like something a real cowgirl would wear," she whispered. "Doesn't it?"

MONTANA MAVERICKS

Dear Reader,

A dream vacation... What do those words mean to you? To some it might mean a cruise to a tropical island. Or a house on an endless beach. Or even a trip to some exotic, far-off city.

Not too many people would think of the tiny town of Rust Creek Falls, but that's exactly where Gemma Chapman planned not just a vacation, but a honeymoon. And when her engagement ends short of a walk down the aisle, Gemma's reservation turns into a honeymoon for one! What's a suddenly single city girl supposed to do in a Western town? Good thing for Gemma, rancher Hank Harlow is there to show her the ropes.

Staying at Maverick Manor is *not* a dream vacation for Hank, but it's where his daughter wants to spend the first week of her summer vacation. When Janie tries to play matchmaker between her dad and Gemma, the divorced single father fears he doesn't stand a chance with the sophisticated city girl. Little does he know that Gemma has always had a thing for cowboys!

What starts out as a vacation romance quickly turns into more. Not only does Hank offer Gemma a true Wild West experience, he also helps her discover her own connection to Rust Creek Falls and a missing piece of her past. But when the honeymoon is over, will Gemma and Hank go back to their real lives, or will they take a chance that a summer fling can blossom into a love for all seasons?

I hope you enjoy Hank and Gemma's story! I always love hearing from readers at stacyconnelly@cox.net or on Facebook!

Hope you all have a summer to remember and maybe even a dream vacation this year!

Stacy Connelly

The Maverick's Summer Sweetheart

—

Stacy Connelly

HARLEQUIN® SPECIAL EDITION

Special thanks and acknowledgment to
Stacy Connelly for her contribution to the
Montana Mavericks continuity.

PLEASE RECYCLE
THIS PRODUCT IS RECYCLABLE

Recycling programs
for this product may
not exist in your area.

ISBN-13: 978-1-335-57389-6

The Maverick's Summer Sweetheart

Copyright © 2019 by Harlequin Books S.A.

Printed in U.S.A.

HARLEQUIN®
TM www.Harlequin.com

Stacy Connelly has dreamed of publishing books since writing stories about a girl and her horse. Eventually, boys made it onto the page as she discovered a love of romance novels. She is thrilled that her novel *Once Upon a Wedding* was recently turned into a movie titled *Christmas Wedding Planner*.

Stacy lives in Arizona with her two spoiled dogs. She loves to hear from readers at stacyconnelly@cox.net, at stacyconnelly.com or on Facebook.

Books by Stacy Connelly

Harlequin Special Edition

Hillcrest House

The Best Man Takes a Bride
How to Be a Blissful Bride

Furever Yours

Not Just the Girl Next Door

The Pirelli Brothers

His Secret Son
Romancing the Rancher
Small-Town Cinderella
Daddy Says, "I Do!"
Darcy and the Single Dad
Her Fill-In Fiancé

Visit the Author Profile page
at Harlequin.com for more titles.

To all the Montana Maverick authors and readers
who have been a part of this series for decades!
I am so happy to join you.

Chapter One

"This is awesome! Don't you think so, Dad?"

As rancher Hank Harlow reluctantly handed over the keys for his classic Ford pickup to the valet and watched a uniformed kid roughly half his age and half his size carry his own luggage toward the impressive entrance of Maverick Manor, he had to admit it sure was different.

Not that Hank had *never* stayed in a fancy hotel before. He had—even if that one time had been on his honeymoon. He didn't spend much time thinking of that long-ago weekend. It was over...as was his marriage.

"Dad!" His preteen daughter, Janie, turned back with an exasperated sigh that only preteen daughters seemed capable of. Standing in front of the iron-trimmed double doors, she threw her arms out wide. "Did you even hear me? Isn't this awesome?"

Dad... That was what Hank thought was awesome. His little girl still calling him "Dad" even though she, like the rest of the tiny town of Rust Creek Falls, Montana, now knew the truth.

With a last glance back at the disappearing bumper of his F-150, Hank jogged over to his daughter. "You are right, kiddo. This place is awesome."

Hugging Janie to his side, he stepped into the lobby. Hank was familiar with the local hotel and its unique story. The timber-and-stone mansion was once a private home locals referred to as Bledsoe's Folly. For years the place had stood empty and abandoned, until Nate Crawford had turned it into the fanciest hotel for miles around. Perched on a mountainside with gorgeous views of the town below, the hotel was a prime location for parties and special events.

But this would be Hank's first time as a guest. And not just for an overnight stay. Nope. When Hank asked Janie how she wanted to spend her first week of summer vacation, this was his daughter's request—a stay at Maverick Manor.

He didn't get it. He really didn't. Staying in a hotel in their own hometown? Sleeping in a strange bed, living out of a suitcase, using ridiculously tiny travel toiletries? All less than thirty miles from the Bar H, his ranch and Janie's home away from home when she wasn't living with her mother and Anne's new husband, Daniel Stockton.

She's growing up, Hank, Anne had told him. *She wants to experience new things.*

Over the past several years, Hank had suffered through quite a few new things—including his divorce, the return of Anne's first love, her remarriage, Janie calling another man *Dad*...

Yeah, he'd had enough of new at a time when he wanted nothing more than to hang on to the way things used to be.

Janie has been missing Abby, Anne had added. *She's feeling a bit disconnected from her best friend, who's off having all these exciting adventures. Janie wants to be seen as mature and sophisticated, too.*

Hank had bitten his tongue at that. Janie had just completed the sixth grade. No one in the sixth grade needed to feel mature or sophisticated. Certainly not his tomboy daughter! But Anne might have a point when it came to Janie's best friend. Abby's mother, Marissa, had married Autry Jones, and since then the family had been living in Paris, where Autry worked for his family's company. Hank supposed Paris did seem new and exciting compared to little ol' Rust Creek Falls, where everyone knew everyone else.

And if staying at Maverick Manor was what Janie wanted, then Hank would make sure this summer vacation was everything his daughter hoped it would be.

"So, what do you want to do first, Janie?" he asked as they waited in line to check in.

Janie grinned up at him. "I want to check out the room and the view. Oh, and then order room service and see what movies are showing and—"

Hank nodded at his daughter's unbridled enthusiasm and tried not to think how the views from the Bar H were the best around or how he and Janie could have shared snacks and watched her favorite flicks right from the comfort of their very own couch.

She'll be a teenager in a few months, Hank, he could hear Anne telling him. *She won't be a little girl forever.*

Not forever. At the rate things were changing, not even for long. As he forced a smile at the woman behind the desk, Hank tried hard not to look into a future where he'd be sitting on that couch, watching movies and eating popcorn…alone.

* * *

Gemma Chapman eyed her reflection in the full-length mirror. The black satiny bikini she'd found in a 5th Avenue boutique had been exactly what she was looking for three months ago. A little sexy, a little revealing, perfect for grabbing her groom's attention on their honeymoon.

Now she didn't know what she'd been thinking.

Discovering only weeks before the wedding that the man she had planned to marry had been sleeping with her best friend had Gemma questioning everything.

Including swimwear.

On paper—like in their engagement announcement and the photo taken by one of New York's most in-demand wedding photographers—she and Chad Matthews had been perfect for each other. Both of them came from affluent families. Both of them had attended prestigious prep schools before going to Ivy League colleges. Gemma worked in the financial district at an investment company, while Chad was already a junior member at a top law firm. They knew the same people and were members at the same club. They both enjoyed an evening at the theater and dining at the trendiest restaurants, followed by a night on the town. And if Gemma had ever longed for something more, her mother was always there to remind her not only how to act, but how to feel.

You should feel honored your stepfather wants to adopt you.

You should feel fortunate Chesterton Prep has accepted you.

You should feel thrilled your stepfather arranged an interview with Carlston, Landry and Greer.

You should feel so excited that Chad proposed.

Walking in on her fiancé and her best friend, Gemma hadn't needed anyone to tell her how she should feel.

Angry…betrayed…humiliated… Certainly she had felt all of that, but shouldn't she have also felt *heartbroken*? And how was it that a relationship that looked so perfect on the outside could end up being so empty inside?

Chad's infidelity had made Gemma start to question what else in her life wasn't as perfect as it seemed. And while her mother was certain Gemma would feel completely miserable on a honeymoon by herself, she had kept her first-class reservation and had arrived in Rust Creek Falls earlier that day.

Unlike her cheating scumbag of an ex, Maverick Manor was exactly as advertised. The bathroom had had all the amenities of a modern hotel but with an added old-fashioned flair in the enormous claw-foot tub and a raised sink reminiscent of a water basin. And though the spacious bedroom—with its hand-scraped wood floors and exposed-beam ceiling—had the same rugged and handcrafted design as the rest of the hotel, the honeymoon suite also boasted a faux-bearskin rug that was spread out in front of a river-rock fireplace and a four-poster bed draped with a sheer white canopy. Romantic touches a newlywed couple would expect.

Which was all the more reason to leave the suite behind and head for the pool.

From what Gemma had seen on her way to her room, the hotel's newly constructed pool looked exactly as it had in the website photos—with rock walls and a waterfall and a spa built to resemble a natural hot spring. The wide wall of windows looked out onto a breathtaking mountain view, and the huge glass panels that could be closed during colder months were open for the summer.

Ignoring the swimsuit for a moment, Gemma adjusted the beaded headband holding back her shoulder-length black hair and eyed the makeup she'd touched up after the long flight. Just a few swipes of mascara on her darkly lashed green eyes and a hint of peachy lip gloss. She was, after all, only going down to the pool. Not that she actually planned to get *in* the pool—at least not more than dipping her manicured feet into the shallow end.

Realizing she was simply wasting time, she finally muttered, "Oh, get over yourself!" The swimsuit wasn't *that* revealing, and she had the white terry-cloth hotel robe to take with her.

She hadn't come all this way to sit in her room, feeling sorry for herself. She could have done that back in her New York apartment. But this was Montana. A land of wide-open spaces, majestic mountains and towering trees. And Rust Creek Falls had been calling to her since she'd first stumbled across the name of the town, a piece of a puzzle that Gemma hoped might fit into one of the empty places in her childhood.

If nothing else, she wanted to experience what might have been. And in the process, she wanted to wipe all the *poor Gemma* thoughts from everyone's minds.

Starting with her own.

Before heading down to the pool, Gemma had packed her tote with half a dozen or so brochures she'd picked up in the lobby—touting everything from the local bar and donut shop, to nearby hiking and camping sites, to a place called Sunshine Farm, which had been dubbed "The Lonelyhearts Ranch" after people who stayed there started finding their true loves.

For the past several months, Gemma had scoured the internet, trying to learn all she could about Rust Creek Falls. She'd been fascinated to discover a blog written by a former New Yorker who had arrived after a devastating flood several years ago. Lissa Roarke's description of the location and the way the community had pulled together in the face of such adversity had added another layer to Gemma's curiosity about the tiny town.

She wasn't sure how long she'd been down by the pool, the shrieks of laughter echoing through a space filled with the scent of sunscreen and chlorine, before she became aware of the young girl dripping by the side of her chair.

"Is that the latest edition?" the girl asked, pointing to the glossy magazine on Gemma's lounger. "The one with the article about Lyle? You know, the former singer of 2LOVEU?"

Sixty-hour workweeks, with her reading material limited to *The Wall Street Journal* and endless finance articles, threatened to make Gemma a dull girl. She did her best to balance all those facts and figures she needed to know in her job as a financial adviser by focusing on the lifestyles of the rich and famous in her free time. And now that she was on vacation, she was far more interested in which super couple was breaking up than in what stock might be splitting.

"I think it is."

"Oh, my gosh!" the girl gushed as she plopped down onto the seat next to Gemma's. "I've been dying to read that. Crawford's General Store is *sooo* slow about getting the newest issues. I actually saw Lyle back when he was in 2LOVEU. My best friend, Abby, and I went to Seattle to see him in concert there. It was the most exciting night of my life!"

Five minutes ago, Gemma wouldn't have thought she had anything to talk about with a girl who was maybe ten? Eleven? But she quickly found herself charmed by the tiny blonde's enthusiasm. She was all skinny arms and legs in a navy polka dot halter-style top and matching boy shorts, and her light blue eyes were already a little red-rimmed from her time in the pool. But the girl had an outgoing smile and confidence Gemma hadn't mastered until she was in her late teens.

"I saw him once, too, when he was on his solo tour in New York City."

"No! Really? Are you from New York? That must be so exciting! I've lived here, like, my whole life! My name's Janie. If there's anything you want to know about Rust Creek Falls, I can totally tell you all about it. Like the time Brenna and Travis starred on *The Great Roundup*—you know, the reality show on TV?"

"You actually know the couple who married in the show's finale?" Gemma hadn't seen the program when it originally aired, but she'd come across it in her search of Rust Creek Falls. When she'd learned two of the cast members were from the small town, she'd binge-watched the entire season, eager to learn who won the grand prize—and whether the couple had hooked up just for ratings or if they had fallen in love for real.

"I do. I know just about everyone in town!"

Janie's eager boast was enough for Gemma to take the words with a grain of salt, but she still had to wonder. If the town truly was that close-knit, then maybe…

Gemma didn't mean to tune out the girl's happy chatter as her thoughts started to wander, but with a glance across the far side of the pool, her attention instantly snapped back to the present. All exhaustion from the months of planning the "wedding that wasn't" fled as her heart slammed in her chest and every nerve ending came to vibrant life at the sight of a gorgeous guy lifting himself out of the deep end. Though she knew it had to be her imagination, he almost seemed to be moving in some kind of super-sexy slow motion. Water sluiced off his broad shoulders and chest, down six-pack abs and along equally muscular legs as he rose to stand on the concrete decking.

She had seen plenty of buff, good-looking guys at the gym where she worked out, but this guy—no, this *man*—was different. He was more rugged and real, and with the mountains as a backdrop behind him, Gemma had the split-second fantasy that this could be an honest-to-goodness cowboy. Certainly there was nothing manscaped or metrosexual about him. As he shook the water from his brown hair and then raised both hands to push it back from his wide forehead, she caught sight of a few faded scars—one thin line along the underside of his tanned forearm and another ragged lightning bolt running down the length of his lean rib cage.

No way did those muscles come from a gym.

As he reached for a towel hanging over the back of a nearby lounge chair, he glanced over and his dark blue eyes met Gemma's gaze. She knew she should look away—she really did—but once he started running that towel down the length of his arms and across that wide chest…

She couldn't even blink, let alone find a way to break her mesmerized stare.

A slow smile broke over his handsome features, crinkling the crow's-feet at the corners of his eyes and warming Gemma from the inside out. She felt almost pinned in place on the pale blue lounger as a small shiver raced from the top of her head, all the way down to her purple-painted toenails.

As she watched, he lifted his fingers toward his lips. He wasn't actually going to blow her a kiss, was he? That certainly didn't seem like a cowboy thing to do. Tip an imaginary hat, maybe, but not—

The thought had barely formed in her mind when the man did indeed raise his fingers to his mouth—to give a shrill, sharp whistle that echoed through the enclosed space and had the young girl on the lounger next to Gemma's giving a slight start.

Janie's chatter cut off abruptly as she glanced across the pool toward the man who now had those impressive arms crossed over his equally impressive chest. Janie's shoulders slumped slightly. "That's my dad."

"Your dad?" Gemma didn't know why the statement surprised her. She would have guessed the man was in his late thirties, possibly early forties. Certainly old enough to be Janie's father.

Somehow, though, her fantasy cowboy hadn't come with a preteen daughter.

"Yeah. He's always watching over me. It's like he doesn't know I'm *practically* a teenager already," she added with an eye roll. "I better go see what he wants."

With that, Janie bounced up from the lounge chair and rushed over to her father's side. He grinned down at his petite daughter, love written in every rugged line of his face, as he listened to the young girl whose hands were moving almost as fast as her mouth.

Of course. That broad smile had been for Janie, not for Gemma.

The gorgeous maybe-cowboy was a dad with a cute blonde daughter and no doubt an equally cute blonde wife.

And Gemma felt like the world's biggest fool. Again.

"Dad! You've got to meet Gemma!"

Hank grinned at Janie's enthusiasm as he draped the damp towel over the back of a chair. Her blue eyes were bright with excitement, despite being a little red from all the chlorine, and he decided that maybe this vacation wasn't such a bad idea after all.

Once they'd checked in the day before, they had explored the hotel a bit, making plans for the next several days. That morning, they had hiked the trails around the hotel before having a late lunch in the dining room. After waiting half an hour—because, yes, he was that kind of dad—they changed into swimsuits and hit the pool.

Hank couldn't remember the last time he'd had a day to relax. The Bar H had a capable foreman who could run the ranch in his absence, but Hank was not a weekend cowboy. His typical days, especially when Janie was at her mother's, consisted of waking before dawn and working until he was ready to drop.

Sleeping in and spending an afternoon by the pool with Janie were luxuries he appreciated far more than any of the hotel's other high-class amenities. Of course, he wasn't sure what they were going to do tomorrow or the next day or the day after that.

One day of lazing around was about all he could take, and he was already anticipating his daughter growing bored. But so far Janie was having a good time, and if she'd made a little friend, it would help her to have someone to play with.

"Where is she?"

"Da-ad." His daughter rolled her eyes in sheer exasperation. "Didn't you see me talking to her right over there?"

She pointed in the direction of the stunning brunette a man would have to be dead not to notice. "That's Gemma?"

Janie nodded. "She's from New York City! Isn't that cool? Did you see the headband she's wearing and how it totally matches her flip-flops? And her tote bag? I bet she bought it at some super-famous store in New York."

Headband? Flip-flops? Bag? No, no and...no. Hank hadn't paid attention to any of those things and was a little surprised that his tomboy daughter had. Which wasn't to say he hadn't locked in on other details about the woman. Like the long black hair shimmering in a sleek wave down her back. The stunning green eyes were so bright, they seemed to glow from within. And when she slid the hotel robe from her shoulders to reveal a barely there bikini that highlighted her slender curves, Hank had found himself wishing the pool wasn't heated. He could have used an instant ice bath to cool the sudden desire burning through his veins.

All of which was so unlike him.

"You've gotta meet her, Dad!" Janie insisted as she tugged on his arm.

"Janie, she's here on vacation. You shouldn't be bothering her."

"I wasn't, Dad. She's all by herself."

A woman like that on a vacation for one? She had to have a husband or boyfriend she was planning to meet up with later. And even if she didn't, Hank had a type, and the women who fit the mold were ones like his ex-wife, Anne. Pretty and sweet in a girl-next-door kind of way.

Janie was right about this woman. She was all big-city style and sophistication. And gorgeous or not, crazy spark or not, New York City was a helluva lot of doors away from Rust Creek Falls.

Even so, Hank reluctantly allowed Janie to drag him across the damp concrete decking, toward the woman reclining on the pale blue lounge chair. For a split second, he thought he saw the brunette's eyes widen ever so slightly and drop to his naked chest as he approached.

Checking him out?

Naw, that had to be his imagination playing games with him.

"Gemma, this is my dad, Hank Harlow," Janie said with enough pride in her voice to have his neck heating slightly. "Dad, this is Gemma..."

"Chapman." Swinging those long, lovely legs over the side of the lounger, Gemma leaned forward to hold out her hand. A half a dozen or so slender gold bracelets jingled as they slid down her arm.

Hank had always considered himself something of a gentleman, but it was hard to know where to look when all that female flesh was on display. Bathing suits were a rarity in Montana, and though she was hardly the only one wearing a bikini, no other woman at the Maverick Manor pool wore one quite so well.

The black satin was a stark contrast to her creamy skin, the narrow straps cutting across her collarbones and molding to the curves of her breasts. Her stomach was smooth and flat, the indentation of her hip bones hollowing out ever so slightly right where the bikini bottom stretched across her belly. Her waist was slender enough that he could likely span it with both hands, and just the thought of feeling that smooth skin sliding against his palms had Hank breaking out into a sweat.

Long-ingrained manners had him taking her hand, instantly registering the delicate bones, as he gruffly murmured, "Miz Chapman."

A small half smile curved her lips, and that heat started spreading out from his neck until his whole body felt on fire. "Please, call me Gemma."

"Gemma..." Realizing he'd been holding on for far too long as he ran his thumb across her silky-smooth skin, he practically jerked his hand away from hers. He lifted his arm, wishing for his old and familiar hat to hide behind, and had to settle for running his fingers through his too long, damp hair instead. "Nice to meet you. Hope Janie here hasn't been talking your ear off."

As expected, his daughter gave a huffing sigh, one that had Gemma's smile widening. "Not at all. She's been keeping me company."

Was Janie right? Could Gemma be vacationing alone? Interest and anticipation buzzed along his nerve endings even as Hank dismissed the possibility. Okay, so maybe he had thought a time or two about jumping back in the dating pool, but this... This would be like launching right off Owl Rock and into the rushing waterfall that gave the town its name. He'd be in over his head the moment he hit water.

"I was telling my dad how you're from New York. And— Oh!" Janie's eyes widened as she grabbed hold of his hand. "Gemma...have you seen the new Disney musical on Broadway?"

Hank tried not to groan. Ever since Janie's favorite actress had left her hit television series to pursue a stage career, his daughter had been obsessed with New York.

"Have I seen it?"

Gemma rose to her feet, and Hank realized she was taller than he first thought, the top of her head coming right to his chin. The perfect height for holding her in his arms. Not that Hank had any intention of testing out that theory.

He was a small-town single dad who hadn't been on a date in well over a decade. Besides, if he needed a visual reference for the phrase *out of his league*, Gemma Chapman would be it.

"I love going to the theater," she was saying, "and that's one of my favorite musicals."

"I know all the songs," Janie boasted.

"Which one do you like best?"

This time Hank didn't bother holding back the groan. One Gemma clearly heard as she shot him a look. Her dewy lips pressed together, trying to hide a smile, as his beautiful, smart, talented and completely tone-deaf daughter started belting out the Oscar-winning song.

A few people in nearby lounge chairs glanced over, but Janie didn't care. Obviously Gemma didn't either, as she too started to sing. Thanks to Janie, Hank had heard the song and seen the DVD numerous times, and the words—like the melody—had been little more than background noise.

But Gemma didn't sing the lyrics so much as she seemed to embrace them. No keeping it in, no holding back…just letting it go. And as she lifted her head, her long dark hair trailing down her slender back, something inside Hank sparked to life. Something that had been, well, frozen for far too long.

Get a grip, Harlow! You're way too old to be taking life lessons from Disney.

By the big finale, the people around them gave a round of applause that had Gemma laughing breathlessly. Even though a bloom of color brightened her cheeks, she brazened out the sudden attention and gave a graceful curtsy, one that Janie immediately copied.

"This afternoon's entertainment has been brought to you by Janie and Gemma," Gemma added with all the flourish of an MC hosting an awards ceremony.

"That was awesome!" Janie practically bounced on her bare toes in her excitement.

"Janie's right. That was…awesome," Hank echoed. The blush in Gemma's cheeks deepened as their gazes met and held, but just like she had with the unexpected applause, she didn't back down. Awareness rippled between them, and Hank wasn't sure when he had moved, but he suddenly noticed a puddle of water from his navy trunks had formed at his feet and was inching toward Gemma's purple-painted toes and sequined flip-flops.

Who wore sequins at a pool?

He took a stumbling step back to keep from dripping on her fancy shoes, nearly tripping over the lounger behind him. He'd barely caught his balance when Janie added, "I totally wanted to go to New York to see the musical, but we'd already booked the hotel here. I'm hoping I can go later this summer with my other dad."

"Other dad?" At that, Gemma's dark brows winged upward as she gave him a somewhat-surprised look.

His face already burning, Hank quickly said, "My ex-wife remarried a year and a half ago."

"Ah, I see."

Did she? Somehow Hank doubted it. Not that he was about to explain that Dan Stockton was more than simply Janie's stepdad. The man was in fact Janie's biological father. And the daughter Hank had raised from birth—the baby girl he'd held in his arms when she was only minutes old, the one he'd rocked into the wee hours of the morning when she was sick or teething, the one who'd taken her first stumbling steps while holding on to his thumbs—was not actually his.

And neither was the woman he'd been married to.

In reality Hank had been little more than a placeholder in Anne's life. A second-best substitute who had stepped in at a time when she had been alone and afraid. From the start Anne had been completely honest. She'd told him all about Daniel Stockton, the young man she had been in love with since high school. How she had thought they would be together forever, how he had disappeared after his parents were killed in a car accident and how she was pregnant with his child.

Hank had asked Anne to marry him anyway, believing in time she would forget about Dan. He'd been so sure that if he took care of her and treated her right, eventually she would grow to love him. And Anne had said yes, certain Dan Stockton was never coming back to Rust Creek Falls.

In the end, though, they'd both been wrong.

Chapter Two

"What else do you like to do, Janie?" Gemma asked. "Other than sing?"

Sitting across a table loaded with chips, popcorn and soft drinks, Hank gave a wry half smile. She had a feeling their impromptu duet had embarrassed him, but he hadn't let it show, praising his daughter's efforts...if not her actual talent.

A completely different reaction to how Gemma's own mother and stepfather would have responded. In Diane and Gregory Chapman's socially structured mind, everything had a time and a place. Performing on stage at a carefully orchestrated and choreographed pageant or school performance was one thing. Singing a cappella poolside was something else.

Her mother would have been mortified, and Gemma didn't even have to try hard to picture how the disappointment and disapproval would have pulled at the features so similar to her own. When Gemma wasn't struggling to rub the image of Chad and Melanie from the inside of her eyelids, she was trying to forget her mother's reaction when she called off the wedding.

Think of the embarrassment, Gemma!

Because, yes, the real scandal was Gemma calling off the wedding weeks before her walk down the aisle. Not her fiancé's sleeping with her best friend.

But to her mother and stepfather, her engagement to Chad had been about more than two people pledging to forsake all others. The wedding would also have united the Chapman and Matthews families. Gemma had no doubt her business-minded stepfather had viewed it in terms of a merger rather than as a marriage. A check mark in the asset column of some mental balance sheet Gregory Chapman kept. To him, the boarding schools and etiquette lessons were finally paying off since Gemma caught the eye of one of NYC's most eligible bachelors.

Determined not to think of the embarrassment, of her broken engagement or her mother, Gemma focused her attention on Janie…and on Hank.

Janie had already asked dozens of rapid-fire questions about Gemma's life—where she worked, where she lived, where she shopped, if she knew anyone famous. It didn't seem to matter much what answer Gemma gave; Janie still thought everything about New York was the most exciting thing ever.

Her father certainly seemed harder to impress. Money, clothes, fame… None of that had the somewhat-silent man seated across from her raising so much as an eyebrow. Not that Gemma was trying to impress him… Was she?

Certainly it would be much easier to regain a bit of equilibrium if Hank wasn't so impressive without even trying. He'd pulled a faded T-shirt on, but the soft blue cotton only molded to those broad shoulders, the sleeves hugging a pair of well-defined biceps. His thick brown hair had dried with a bit of a wave, the too-long locks falling across his wide forehead and curling at the strong column of his neck.

On another man, the tousled hair might have looked boyish or at least done something to soften his masculine features. On Hank, it only drew attention to his rugged features and the solid set of his jaw.

There was nothing boyish or soft about Hank Harlow.

Gemma didn't think he was trying for any kind of fashion statement. More likely he was a month or two beyond needing a haircut. But instead of being turned off by the overgrown style, she longed to run her hands through a man's hair without worrying about encountering more product than she put in her own.

So distracted by the tempting fantasy, Gemma almost forgot the question she asked by the time Janie stated, "I love to go horseback riding."

Horseback riding… Gemma had never been on a horse.

At least not that she remembered.

Many years ago, when she had been around Janie's age, Gemma had found an old picture of herself as a toddler. In the photo, she'd been stumbling toward the camera in a red bandanna-print shirt and denim overalls, with a pink cowboy hat on her head and a pair of fawn-colored boots on her feet.

The picture and the outfit had stood out in such sharp contrast to the typical professional shots of Gemma in frilly, girlie dresses that—as the overly imaginative child she'd been and thanks to a Disney remake she'd just seen—she had been convinced the girl in the photo was her separated-at-birth twin sister.

Her mother, who evidently had not seen either version

of the motion picture, had shaken her head in exasperation. "Honestly, Gemma, I don't know where you come
up with these ideas. That is a picture of you at some Hal-
loween party or playing dress up."

Though disappointed, Gemma had believed her mother.
But after finding a box of mementos while looking for
"something old" for her wedding, she'd started to wonder.
Not about some imaginary long-lost sibling, but about her
long-lost father. She'd started feeling more and more like
the designer suits and latest fashions she wore were the
costumes, hiding a completely different person inside.

Two weeks wasn't much time to discover her inner
cowgirl, but Gemma was determined to try.

"Horseback riding is definitely on my list," she stated.

"Your list?" Hank echoed.

Gemma nodded. "My vacation to-do list."

"You have a to-do list for your vacation? I thought the
whole point of a vacation was not having to do anything."

"I want to experience everything I can. To find out
what life in Rust Creek Falls is all about."

At that, Hank gave a slight snort. "This is not what
Rust Creek Falls is all about."

He waved a hand, and in an instant she could feel his
palm against hers once more. The work-roughened skin,
the slight rise of hardened calluses, the strong fingers.
Such a contrast to the sensual, almost seductive stroke
of his thumb across the back of her hand when they'd
shaken hands earlier, and the memory alone had goose-
flesh racing up her arm. "This is a hotel."

"A hotel in Rust Creek Falls," she pointed out.

"Where all the city folks stay when they're wanting
a 'real Western experience.'" With a nod toward the art-
fully crafted rock waterfall pouring into the crystal clear

pool, he added, "But there isn't much *real* or even Western about this place. Other than its location."

Of course the hotel would be for tourists—city folks, as Hank had so plainly pointed out—like her. But even if he was right, the hotel was simply a place to stay. And besides... "Janie told me she's lived here her whole life, and you don't exactly strike me as 'city folk.'"

She lowered her voice to mimic Hank's deep drawl, drawing an instant giggle from Janie. He shot his daughter a mock scowl before reaching over and tousling her damp blond hair. The simple father-daughter exchange grabbed hold of a decades-old longing in Gemma's heart.

"This is a vacation for us, too," he said finally. "A chance to get *away* from real life in Rust Creek Falls for a week. But then we'll head back home and everything will be back to the way it was before."

As Hank glanced over at her and their gazes caught, a very different kind of longing took over. Was there some message Gemma should read into that statement? Something along the lines of *what happens at Maverick Manor...*

Not that Gemma was in any shape to even think of dating, something her heart and her brain were in complete agreement about. Her body, though, had other ideas. Despite his views on "city folk," she was way too attracted to Hank Harlow. More than his rugged good looks, she was drawn to his deep drawl, subtle humor and slightly old-fashioned manners.

And while Hank was right that the setting might not have been authentically Western, the swift rush of attraction racing through her certainly fell under the heading of *wild*.

After taking a swallow of raspberry-flavored iced tea to soothe her suddenly dry throat, Gemma did her best to direct her thoughts back to where they belonged. "I picked up some brochures in the lobby about the horseback-riding tours around town. Is there a certain stable you go to when you want to ride?"

Janie giggled again, and Gemma noticed the quick look the girl exchanged with her father. "Um, yeah, the stables at our ranch."

"Ranch?" No wonder Hank didn't think much about imitation waterfalls and guided trail rides set up through a concierge. She turned to him. "So, you're a real cowboy?"

"As opposed to the fake kind?" he asked.

"As opposed to… Oh, I don't know." The truth was, she knew pathetically little about any kind of cowboy—real or fake. But she certainly knew plenty about men who weren't who they pretended to be.

"He's not a cowboy. He's a rancher," Janie corrected, the voice of authority. "This is his first vacation in, like, forever. The Bar H is a cattle ranch, and my dad runs the whole place."

Gemma noticed a slight smile on Hank's lips as he listened to his daughter go on. The same smile had been on his face when he'd praised Janie's singing. Clearly he was indulging the girl and didn't want to correct her exaggerations. Dozens of horses? Hundreds of cattle? Ten thousand acres? Janie must have meant *one thousand*, though Gemma found even that number hard to imagine.

Still, it was sweet the way he was humoring the young girl, and one thing that wasn't overstated was Janie's pride and love for her father. The refrain that had haunted Gemma's childhood whispered through her mind once more as she contemplated the love Hank clearly held in return for his daughter.

What if…?

Shifting in his chair, Hank said, "All right, Janie, enough. Gemma doesn't want to hear about all that." Beneath that rancher's tan, a hint of embarrassed color was darkening his cheekbones.

"But Gemma said she wanted to go horseback riding and— Hey, Dad, you should take her!"

Now it was Gemma's turn to feel uncomfortable. "Oh, Janie, that's sweet of you to offer, but your dad's here on vacation. With you."

"I know, but I'm signed up for all kinds of stuff through the hotel this week. My dad's not. He'll be all alone."

Gemma glanced over at Hank, expecting another half grin at his daughter's somewhat-dramatic statement. Only he wasn't smiling, and Gemma realized the truth in his daughter's words. The slight reticence she sensed about him was more than the rancher's simply being the strong, silent type. This was a man who'd been hurt in the past.

Was it the divorce? His ex-wife's remarriage? Was he still in love with her?

Gemma's heart cramped a little at the thought, even though the feeling—any feeling for this man—was pre-posterous. They didn't even know each other and had barely exchanged more than a few words. And though he hadn't come straight out and said so, he'd made his views on city folks crystal clear. But if Gemma wanted to truly experience Rust Creek Falls, having a local as a guide *would* help. And if he happened to be a gorgeous cowboy with eyes as blue as Montana's Big Sky, well, that certainly wouldn't hurt!

"I'm sure Gemma can find a trail guide who can take her riding," Hank told his daughter.

"But, Dad!"

Gemma was glad for Janie's instant objection as it kept her from making one of her own. She didn't want some hired tour guide. She wanted…

Oh, no. Not going there, Gem!

"You *have* to take her. You're the best!" Janie was saying.

Hank opened his mouth, but Gemma beat him to the punch. "I did come all the way to Montana for my very first horseback ride. Seems only right that I should have the chance to learn from the best."

As Gemma held Hank's gaze, that same small shiver of awareness raced down her spine. She didn't know what was happening between the two of them, but she couldn't shake the feeling that for a city girl from Manhattan and a Montana cowboy—sorry, make that Montana rancher—she and Hank Harlow had more in common than anyone might think.

"Is that what you're wearing to dinner tonight?" Janie asked as Hank stepped out of his side of the suite. The room was decorated with the same upscale Western decor as the rest of the hotel—all warm shades of rust and brown, hardwood floors, rough-hewn furniture and even a river-rock fireplace in the shared living space between the two bedrooms.

His daughter was seated on the couch, parked in front of the oversize television, remote in hand. But she flicked the television show off as she pushed to her feet and eyed him with a frown.

Hank glanced down, trying to see what had his little girl making that face. His long-sleeved checkered shirt was buttoned properly, his brown leather belt was pulled through all the loops and his dark denim jeans were zipped.

"What else would I wear?" he asked his daughter. He could dress in the dark, pulling clothes from his closet while completely blind, and end up with an outfit exactly like the one he had on.

Short-sleeved button-down shirts for summer, long

sleeves for spring and fall, and a few sweaters thrown in for winter, along with his leather duster. Add in his most comfortable boots and his favorite hat, and there wasn't a place in Rust Creek Falls where he wouldn't meet the dress code. That was assuming Rust Creek Falls actually had any restaurants where a dress code was required— which it didn't.

"You should, I don't know, wear a tie or something."

"Now, Janie, you know that I do not own a tie." It was something of a joke between them—how some kids bought ties for Father's Day. Last year Janie had bought him a pair of spurs. The year before that, it had been a snakeskin hatband. Before that she had given him a new pair of work gloves. Always something he could wear, but never, ever a tie.

"I know, but I bet Gemma's gonna dress up."

Hank doubted the big-city beauty knew how to dress down. Even if she tried to fit in, he imagined her hat and boots would be some designer brand and color-coordinated as well. Like the way her purple toenail polish, complete with tiny, delicate painted-on flowers that were practically works of art, had perfectly matched her oversize floral-print tote bag.

It was a ridiculous thing for a grown man to have noticed. Even worse to have his interest caught by such a detail. But like the rest of Gemma Chapman, the delicate, feminine touch fascinated Hank more than he wanted to admit.

He was simply out of practice when it came to the opposite sex. It wasn't like women walked around the Bar H in flip-flops all the time. Hell, it wasn't like many women walked around the Bar H period.

"Sorry, kiddo, but this is the best I brought with me."

Janie sighed. "You're supposed to dress up when you go out on a date."

"Whoa! Hey, no one said anything about this being a date. It's dinner." Between two total strangers who were complete opposites and a preteen chaperone. Although even with those built-in safeguards, Hank wasn't sure why or even how he'd ended up agreeing to share a meal with Gemma Chapman.

The conversation had started out innocently enough when Janie, who always seemed to be starving even though they'd all snacked on chips and popcorn by the pool, asked about their plans for dinner. Or rather Gemma's plans for dinner.

"I was thinking about checking out a place I read about online. I'm guessing the two of you have heard of it. It's called the Ace in the Hole?"

"The Ace?" Gemma Chapman at the local cowboy bar? Alone? On a Saturday night? "Uh, no, ma'am. You don't want to go there."

Her dark eyebrows rose at that—though Hank wasn't sure if the move was in reaction to his slipping and calling her "ma'am" or from telling her not to go. "Why not? It sounded like fun. A real Western experience."

The bar had its moments and was certainly popular enough, but on a Saturday night the place could get more than a little rowdy with just-been-paid and partying cowboys—all of whom would be more than happy to show Gemma a "real Western experience."

"It's just not the place for a woman like you."

"A woman like me?" This time Hank had no doubt his words had sparked her reaction. She tossed that long black hair back in a challenging gesture that reminded Hank of a spirited filly. He doubted a city girl like Gemma would appreciate that comparison, but he did.

Before he knew it, he'd offered to take Gemma—and Janie—to the Ace in the Hole for an early dinner. His plan was for the three of them to get in and get out before the late-night crowd showed up and the music and dancing started.

He didn't want to look too closely at the reasons why the idea of Gemma in another man's arms bothered him. And thinking about her in his own arms... Well, that was equally dangerous territory.

"Okay, okay," Janie was saying, "so it's *just dinner*." His daughter put so much emphasis on the two words, he half expected them to appear over her head in some kind of dialogue bubble. "You should still try to look nice."

Lifting a hand, Hank rubbed at the back of his neck, where his too-long hair brushed well below the collar. Sad thing was, he actually *had* tried to look nice, shaving a second time and trying to get the slight wave in his hair combed back off his forehead. "'Fraid this is as good as it gets, kiddo. But what about you?"

Janie had changed into sweatpants and a long-sleeved T-shirt, her typical movie-night apparel, after her quick shower to wash the chlorine from her hair. "That doesn't look like what you'd want to wear going out to dinner."

"I, um... I'm not feeling that great."

"What's wrong? Was it too many snacks down by the pool? I knew we shouldn't have had chips and popcorn."

Not to mention the refills on the sugary soda. Anne was always warning him about indulging Janie's sweet tooth, but Hank had a hard time resisting—both his daughter as well as his own love of snacks.

Striding toward the hotel phone, he asked, "Should I see if the gift shop has something for an upset stomach?" The tiny space tucked away in the corner of the lobby had the typical tiny travel-sized necessities that guests frequently forgot to pack. Likely the store would have something for a stomachache as well.

"No, Dad, it's not my stomach. It's…my head. Probably just too much sun down by the pool."

"Okay," Hank drawled, not sure how that could be, considering the pool was mostly enclosed, with only muted sunlight streaming through the wall of windows. Janie tugged on the hem of her shirt as her gaze flitted about the room, a sure sign she was fibbing, but why? She'd been the one so gung ho about this dinner. "If you don't feel well, I'll call Gemma's room and cancel—"

"No!" Janie practically shouted before catching herself. "I mean, it would be rude to cancel so late." Sinking down onto the sofa, she pulled a pillow into her lap. "I can just rest here and order room service. But you— you should still go."

This time, as she looked up at him—her sweet face so earnest, so sincere, so eager—Hank knew for a fact she was faking. And the reason why was pretty clear. Janie wasn't interested in dinner for the three of them. She was trying to finagle a dinner between him and Gemma.

So much for his preteen chaperone.

"Janie…,"

Enough warning entered his voice that she at least dropped the wide-eyed expression. "Please, Dad, go! I'll be fine here. One of my favorite movies is on tonight, and I'll order something super healthy like what Mom would make for dinner. And you can go and have fun with Gemma."

Have fun with Gemma…

The image of his future—sitting alone in front of the television—had his denial dying in his throat. Ever since Anne had remarried, Janie—hell, Janie and Anne and half of Rust Creek Falls, it seemed sometimes—had been pushing him to start dating. But his daughter was especially worried about him being by himself. As frequently as he insisted that he was fine, she wasn't buying it.

Fine isn't the same as happy, Hank.

The voice echoing through his mind wasn't his daughter's, but his mother's. Penny Harlow had passed away a few years after Hank's marriage to Anne. Though she had loved her granddaughter and adored her daughter-in-law, Penny had seen then what Hank refused to believe.

You deserve someone who will love you for who you are.

Who he was hadn't been the problem in his marriage. The issue was who he *wasn't.* After five years of marriage, Hank had been forced to face facts. He wasn't Daniel Stockton, the only man Anne would ever—could ever—love.

And if Hank wanted something more out of life than being "just fine" by himself, then he needed to make some kind of effort. Perhaps he could look at Gemma Chapman as a very, very short-term solution. Going out would make Janie happy, and maybe a few evenings with Gemma would be a way of easing back into the dating scene.

At the end of her vacation, Gemma would go back to the big city, and Hank would go back to the Bar H. And then when he did meet a woman who was more of his type than a gorgeous out-of-towner from New York, he would have already gotten his legs back beneath him. He would hopefully be ready to start dating, and he wouldn't have to feel so foolish and nervous and jump-out-of-his-skin uncomfortable. Which was everything he felt and more as he stepped out of the suite and headed for dinner with Gemma Chapman.

Five minutes later and Hank had to admit the evening was off to an inauspicious start. First Janie bailed with what he believed was a phony headache, and now he was starting to wonder if Gemma had given him a fake room number. He'd followed the sequential plaques, but the row of doors ended one shy of the room number Gemma had told him was hers.

A young couple emerged at the end of the hallway, and Hank quickly stepped back, feeling like some kind of stalker lurking outside of their room. But the twenty-somethings didn't even notice him. With their arms wrapped around each other, they were in their own love-filled world as the guy bent to murmur something into the laughing girl's ear. As they made their way toward the lobby, stopping every few feet to kiss beneath the glowing lights of the old-fashioned sconces, Hank wondered why they'd even bothered to leave the room…and if he'd ever been that young.

It certainly didn't feel that way now. By the time he'd been old enough to drink, he'd already been running the family ranch, having taken over following his father's stroke. At a time when many of his friends were off at college or finding themselves by trying out different part-time jobs, Hank's steps had carried him over the well-worn trails that had been carved out by generations of Harlows before him.

For nearly a decade, Hank had done little more than work, eat and sleep, his patterns following that of his cattle as spring calving gave way to fall roundup in the same way that the sun rose and the sun set, and the next thing he'd known, his early twenties were gone and he was pushing thirty.

He'd never minded the long hours, the extreme weather, the backbreaking and sometimes heartbreaking life on the ranch. At the time, he'd believed he was working toward something—50 percent ownership of the Rolling Hills spread, the equal share his father had once owned with Hank's uncle.

But the years of long-term care for his father had taken their toll. A proud man, his father had sold some of his shares to his brother to pay for the in-home assistance he required. After his father's passing, Hank had tried to buy back those shares only to be told by his uncle that they weren't for sale.

Hank had mourned the loss of his father, but he had seen that coming as his father's health had slowly deteriorated. The blow his uncle had landed had blindsided Hank, leaving him reeling as his world was pulled out from beneath him.

Doesn't matter how hard you work or what you think you have to offer. Rolling Hills will never be yours.

So Hank had done what he never thought he would— he sold his uncle what was left of his holdings in the family ranch and walked away. His mother, who had tired of ranch life, had moved with him to Bozeman and settled into a small active adult community. That was about the time when he met Anne, and for a while he'd believed life could be different. After they married, he took his share of the money from selling the ranch and moved to Rust Creek Falls. He bought the Bar H, Janie was born and the three of them were a family.

But just like Rolling Hills, no matter how hard he worked, no matter how much he thought he had to offer, that family wasn't his either. And since the divorce, he'd fallen back into the long hours, pushing himself the way he had when he was in his teens, and ignoring the aches and pains that were his body's way of reminding him that he wasn't a kid anymore.

Ah, hell, one thing he knew for sure was that he was too old for the way his heart was pounding in his chest and his palms were sweating at the thought of seeing Gemma Chapman again. This was a mistake, no doubt about it.

Turning around at the dead end in the hallway, Hank heard the squeak of wheels and spotted a hotel employee pushing a dinner cart his way.

"Excuse me," he said to the young woman. "I'm looking for one of your guests."

The tiny woman's shoulders straightened as she tightened her grip on the handle. "I'm sorry, sir, but it's against hotel policy to divulge any of our guests' room numbers."

Yep, no doubt about it. He was definitely giving off some kind of stalker vibe.

"Sorry—what I meant was that I'm looking for suite 103."

Somehow, knowing Gemma's room number didn't seem to help his cause. The woman drew the cart closer to her as if she thought he was going to abscond with it. He glanced down at the white linen-covered cart decked out with a fancy champagne bottle, two paper-thin crystal flutes, glistening oysters on a bed of ice and a decadent heart-shaped arrangement of chocolate-covered strawberries.

Even if he hadn't been a cattle rancher, Hank would always consider himself a meat and potatoes kind of guy. Just the idea of swallowing the slimy shellfish had his stomach turning. And if he ever actually tried... Well, he was pretty sure something equally disgusting would come back up.

"Suite 103?" she echoed. "The honeymoon suite?"

"The honey—*what*?"

The word caught in Hank's throat as he once again locked in on the over-the-top romantic spread on the cart. This time, though, he caught sight of something he'd missed. A square envelope propped against the ice bucket. The word *congratulations* was written in bright red script across the front. Along with the names of the happy couple...

Gemma and Chad.

Who the hell is Chad?

Even as the question ricocheted around Hank's head, the answer was obvious.

"Yes, sir," the server acknowledged. "Suite 103 is the honeymoon suite. Perhaps you've made a mistake."

There was no *perhaps* about it. Hank didn't know what Gemma Chapman's game was, but he wasn't up for playing the fool.

Chapter Three

"Ms. Chapman?"

Gemma looked up from the scrambled eggs she'd been pushing around her plate to see a tall, good-looking man standing by her table. Unlike just about every guy she'd seen since stepping foot in Rust Creek Falls, this one wore dark trousers and a pale blue button-down shirt, far more business casual than country cowboy.

"Yes?"

"I'm Nate Crawford, the owner here at Maverick Manor."

"Oh." After shaking his hand, she said, "It's a pleasure to meet you. You have a wonderful hotel. It's everything the website promised."

"I'm glad to hear you're enjoying your stay. I, um…" A hint of discomfort crossed his handsome features as he gestured to the empty chair across from her. "Do you mind if I join you for a moment?"

"Please have a seat." Gemma knew small towns had

the reputation for providing a personal touch, but something in Nate Crawford's expression told her this wasn't simply part of the Rust Creek Falls welcome committee. "Is something wrong?"

"Actually, I was going to ask you that question. Or if everything is all right…. If you're comfortable staying in the suite."

"Ah, you mean in the honeymoon suite when I'm technically not on my honeymoon?" Gemma supposed it wasn't that much of a surprise that word had gotten back to Nate that the bride had checked in sans groom. Hoping her cheeks weren't as red as they felt, she reached for her orange juice and took a swallow of the tart citrus, half wishing she'd ordered it mixed with champagne. Or better yet, vodka.

Shifting in the chair, Nate Crawford looked almost as uncomfortable as Gemma felt. "If I had known… We do have guests checking out this afternoon if you would prefer to switch suites. We could have your luggage moved by this evening."

For a split second, Gemma considered making the change before she shook her head. "Thank you for the offer, but I'm fine where I am." After all, she had booked the honeymoon suite months ago, and even though the room was being charged to Chad's credit card, Gemma felt she had more than paid for it.

As he pushed back from the table, Nate Crawford said, "If you change your mind…"

"I won't," Gemma vowed. She was going to hold her head high despite the humiliation of discovering her fiancé had been cheating…as well as being stood up for dinner the night before.

A look of respect entered Nate's green eyes as he gave

a short nod. "If there's anything you need during your stay, please let me know."

"Thank you, but I'm fine by myself."

All by myself.

Gemma knew Janie had somewhat twisted Hank's arm into offering to take her out for dinner, but she never considered that he might not show. On the contrary, nerves had danced in her stomach as she readied for the date. She'd blow-dried her hair using a large-barreled brush to ensure the long dark locks had the perfect shine and played up her green eyes with a smoky mix of brown shadow and two coats of mascara.

Though she had planned this Montana vacation, Gemma didn't have any Western wear. Instead she'd dressed in her NYC finest—a halter-style little black dress with a skirt that ended just above the knee and a pair of strappy heels.

Anticipation had thrummed through her veins as she waited and waited and waited…

It had taken a ridiculously long amount of time before she finally accepted Hank wasn't coming. Perhaps because she'd been so sure he was the type of old-fashioned gentleman she'd given up on finding in New York…or anywhere, for that matter. That he was a *real* cowboy at heart—the kind who was honest and heroic and trustworthy.

But Gemma's taste when it came to men was anything *but* trustworthy. Clearly she'd misjudged Hank Harlow as badly as she had her former fiancé.

And as if the night couldn't get worse, room service had delivered a romantic offering of chilled oysters on the half shell, strawberries and champagne—an unneeded reminder of the wedding that wasn't. No doubt Wilson Montgomery had placed the order after she met with him months ago and had simply forgotten to cancel.

Wilson was her biggest client—and an old Chapman family friend. It wasn't the first time he had sent her a gift basket of some kind, and Gemma had heard the not-so-secretive whispers behind her back. How her stepfather's connections had gotten Gemma the job and how friends like the Montgomerys, rather than the long nights and weekends she worked, were the only reason why she was being considered for promotion.

As the evening grew later, Gemma had been tempted to pop open the champagne bottle and finish it off herself. But she'd refrained. She had, however, devoured the dark chocolate she'd peeled off the strawberries and unceremoniously dumped the oysters—which Chad loved and she hated—into the garbage.

The idea of going to the Ace in the Hole by herself held no appeal, but she'd be damned if she'd let any man—not her cheating ex and not her nonexistent dinner date—ruin this trip for her! So she'd headed to the hotel restaurant, half expecting to see Hank there, wining and dining another woman. After all, wasn't that par for her course lately? But if he had found a better offer, he hadn't taken her to Maverick Manor's dining room.

Afterward she'd returned to her suite and turned in early, her first night on her honeymoon for one as miserable as her friends had warned her it would be…even if not for the reason they would have expected.

Refusing to stay in such a funk, she'd brought her tablet down to the dining room that morning. Of course she couldn't scroll through a single website without finding some reference to trail rides and enjoying the scenic views on horseback. Which meant she couldn't stop thinking about Hank and how excited she'd been at the idea of learning to ride from a genuine Montana cowboy.

It's a state chock-full of cowboys, Gem, she scolded herself. *You can hire any one of them.*

It wouldn't be the same, though, as having Hank teach her.

But even if horseback riding was off the agenda, Gemma had her list of things to do, and nowhere on it was "feel sorry for yourself." Finishing up her breakfast of scrambled eggs and yogurt topped with fresh berries and crunchy granola, she signed the check and pushed away from the table. She draped the strap of her Louis Vuitton bag over her shoulder and was headed from the dining room and into the lobby when she heard Janie call out her name.

Gemma cringed. As much as she'd enjoyed the young girl's company the day before, wherever Janie was, her father was sure to be close by. Forcing a smile, she turned to see the preteen rushing toward her. Dressed in jeans and a checkered shirt, the girl looked exactly how Gemma imagined a Montana rancher's daughter should. But unlike the day before, when a huge smile lit Janie's face, today her blond brows were pulled together in a frown.

Refusing to look over her shoulder to see if her father stood nearby, Gemma focused on Janie. "Hi, Janie. How are you doing this morning?"

"Oh, I'm much better than last night. My headache's totally gone. It's—it's kinda like I never had one in the first place," she all but muttered beneath her breath.

"Headache?" Gemma echoed.

Janie nodded. "Yeah, I told my dad he should still go to dinner with you, but he said he wouldn't have had any fun knowing I was back in the room by myself."

Okay...so a sick kid was certainly a good enough reason for canceling dinner, but why hadn't Hank called to tell her? And why did Janie seem to think Gemma already knew that she hadn't felt well the night before?

"So last night, you and your dad…"

Janie sighed. "Ordered room service and watched a movie. What did you do? Did you end up going to the Ace?"

"I…" *Wasted a ridiculous amount of time getting ready for a date that never happened.* But of course she couldn't say that. "I came down here for dinner and then went back to my room for an early night."

"I'm sorry we didn't get to go to the Ace."

"Yes, so am I." Sorry and confused and entirely unable to keep her gaze on Janie as Hank walked up behind his daughter.

After standing her up last night, Gemma would have liked to believe that Hank Harlow wasn't as good-looking as she remembered. That sun exposure or jet lag or, heck, an overdose of clean mountain air had all conspired against her, making her think the man was better looking than he really was.

If anything, the opposite proved true.

Dressed in well-worn jeans that hugged his thighs and a checkered Western-style shirt that stretched across his broad shoulders, he looked like a cowgirl's dream. Or more precisely a city girl's fantasy, as Gemma couldn't seem to pull her gaze away.

Glancing over her shoulder at her father, Janie said, "Hey, Dad, I was just telling Gemma how we had dinner in our room and watched TV last night."

"Were you?" he asked, his deep voice sending unwarranted—and unwanted—chills down Gemma's spine.

"Uh-huh. You should see our room, Gemma. It's so cool."

"I'm sure Gemma's room is plenty cool," Hank stated flatly. "Probably the fanciest suite in the place."

Gemma lifted a shoulder in a shrug. "Well, it is the..." *Honeymoon suite.*

She didn't say the words, but she could see in Hank's somber gaze that he already knew. Knew and thought *what* exactly? Did he honestly believe she would make plans with another man while she was on her own honeymoon? Even Chad hadn't done something as sleazy as that...though since she'd called off the wedding before the honeymoon, perhaps she'd simply robbed him of the opportunity.

A wave of anger washed over her like molten lava, hot enough to burn away the icy layer of indifference she'd submerged herself in since she'd walked in on Chad and her supposed best friend. She hadn't yelled. She hadn't screamed. A part of her had felt as though she'd flipped on the television to some cheesy reality show about cheating spouses, one where she didn't know—or *care*—enough about the characters for the on-screen drama to matter.

But it wasn't television; it was her *life*. Her fiancé. Her best friend. And she should have cared what was happening because it was happening to *her*! How had everything gotten so screwed up that instead of being devastated by her broken engagement, she'd felt...relieved?

But heartbroken or not, she'd still been humiliated. As she'd taken on the painful task of phoning the guests, canceling the venue, the caterer and the cake, and returning the gaily wrapped presents sent in advance, she couldn't help wondering... How many of Chad's friends, and how many of her friends, had known he was cheating before she did?

So maybe her heart hadn't been broken, but her trust had been—her trust in her fiancé, in her friends, even in her own judgment. How was she supposed to believe in someone else when she no longer believed in herself?

But she'd believed Hank. From the moment they met, she'd sensed he was someone she could trust, a man she could count on. That the cowboy charm and old-fashioned manners were as much a part of him as his gorgeous blue eyes.

And for him to think so little of her… That hurt. Far more than Gemma wanted to admit.

"Janie, can you give me a second to talk to your dad?"

Clearly not picking up on the tension between the two adults, the girl's eyes lit. "Sure! I need to check in at the concierge for today's nature walk anyway, right, Dad?"

"Right, Janie. Come back here when you're done."

"Okay, and maybe you guys can talk about going riding," she suggested as she walked backward through the lobby. "Remember, you promised to teach Gemma!"

Without Janie as a buffer, that tension only increased until Gemma felt as though the air between them was practically crackling. The moment his daughter was out of earshot, Hank mumbled, "I'm sure you have better things to do than going riding."

"Oh, you're sure, are you?" Gemma crossed her arms over her chest as she met his discomforted gaze with a full-on stare down. "Like what, Hank? What better things could I possibly have to do while I'm on my, oh, I don't know, *honeymoon*?"

He glanced around as her voice rose, looking even more pained than he had the day before when she and Janie had started singing. "Look, Gemma—"

"No, you look! Yes, I am staying in the honeymoon suite, but I am not married, and I am not engaged, and you, Hank Harlow, have been watching too much television if you think that just because I'm from the city I'm interested in some kind of kinky, three-way sex!"

Gemma did have the wherewithal to lower her voice as she hissed that final accusation, but she still had the satisfaction of watching a dull flush color his sculpted cheekbones. Hank opened his mouth, closed it and then opened it again.

Finally he said, "I'm not real sure what watching television has to do with anything. Can't tell you the last time I watched much TV other than movies with Janie, but—"

"Hey, Dad!"

Looking grateful for the interruption, Hank turned as Janie rushed back over to them. "What's up?"

"Davey's mom and dad got food poisoning last night." Janie wrinkled her nose. "They were supposed to help chaperone today, so the hotel guide is looking for someone else to volunteer."

"Sure thing, kiddo. I can do that," Hank said.

Gemma ground her back teeth together. And of course he would do something like make a dozen or so kids' day! Why'd he have to go and be such a...such a nice guy at a time when Gemma was still trying so hard to be mad at him?

Jerk.

"Great! I'll go tell Ms. Mitchell that you and Gemma are gonna help out!"

"Whoa, Janie." He glanced over, and something in his expression made Gemma wonder what he saw as he searched her features. The anger she was determined to show...or the hurt she was trying to hide? "You have to remember Gemma's from New York. City girls and nature don't mix."

"Oh, and you're such an expert on city girls, aren't you, Hank?" she muttered beneath her breath. Turning to Janie with a smile, Gemma said, "Tell Ms. Mitchell I'm happy to help chaperone."

As the girl ran off to inform the guide, Gemma turned back to Hank, who met her challenging glare with lifted eyebrows. "What? You really don't think I can manage a nature walk?"

"I think it'll be mighty entertaining watching you try." His blue-eyed gaze took a slow sweep from head to toe, leaving a trail of fire in its wake.

Entertaining? Only as she glanced down at her own feet did Gemma remember the strappy heels she'd put on that morning.

Ones that had "city girl" written all over them.

Last night, as he'd lain wide awake, staring at an unfamiliar ceiling, Hank had told himself he didn't care that Gemma Chapman was—at least as far as *he* was concerned—off-limits. He wasn't looking for a relationship and certainly not with someone so completely his opposite.

But the relief that had rushed through him, leaving him as weak-kneed as a newborn colt at those words— *I am not married, and I am not engaged*—told Hank he cared a damn sight more than he wanted to admit.

But it still didn't answer his question from last night. *Who the hell is Chad?*

Hank still didn't know what the story was, but as a man who took pride in being both honest and fair, his quick judgment and poor treatment of Gemma made him ashamed of himself. His chest tightened a bit at the thought of her sitting in her room—in the damn honeymoon suite, of all places—waiting for him to show up and questioning why he hadn't.

Sure, the romantic room service order had been pretty

damning evidence, but the conclusions he'd jumped to had more to do with him than with Gemma. No doubt left over from his marriage, where he'd spent years looking over his shoulder for the man who would eventually take his place.

He never should have agreed to dinner last night. If he hadn't, it would have saved him—both of them—a bit of misery. Annoyed, irritated and not wanting to admit how disappointed he was over what might have been, Hank rubbed a hand over the back of his neck.

The kids gathered around the front of the hotel were getting equally restless—the boys jostling each other around, while the girls were snapping picture after picture on their cell phones.

Everyone was waiting for Gemma. Because of course a city girl would require a wardrobe change for every occasion.

Low blow, Harlow, his conscience chided. Gemma hadn't planned for a nature walk that morning, and no way could she go on a hike in heels. He didn't even know how she managed to walk across the hotel's patterned carpet without breaking an ankle, but he'd sure as hell enjoyed watching her go. Those killer heels made her legs look a mile long as she'd stalked from the lobby with a determined flick of her long dark hair.

He should have known a woman like Gemma would take his comment about city girls and nature as some kind of dare. Hadn't he intended it that way? A challenge to get Gemma to agree to spend more time with him, when keeping their distance would be best for both of them?

He'd get through chaperoning this nature walk—assuming Gemma ever came back down from the honeymoon suite, and—

"Okay!" the young female guide announced. "Looks like we're all ready to go!"

Hank opened his mouth to protest that they were still waiting for Gemma when a dark, perky ponytail caught his eye. And once he got a good look at the outfit Gemma had changed into, he couldn't have spoken to save his life. He had no doubt the black yoga outfit was some well-known designer label, but that wasn't what had his jaw dropping to his chest.

The sleek material outlined her every curve with such a faithful hand, the pants and matching jacket might as well have been painted on. And when she bent over to do some kind of stretch, he had to drag his gaze away before his eyeballs popped out of his head.

He turned his attention to the Maverick Manor employee as she discussed the route they would take, along with nature-friendly etiquette that included collecting their trash, not picking any of the wildflowers along the trail and keeping their distance from any wildlife they might encounter.

"Um...wildlife?"

A slight waver shook Gemma's voice. Just another reminder that she didn't belong in Rust Creek Falls. She likely wouldn't last five minutes out on the trail.

"It's always a good idea to be aware of your surroundings," the guide was saying. "And with that in mind, we're going to have a buddy system on this hike. So everyone match up two by two!"

Hank instantly looked to Janie, but his bighearted daughter had found her match in a younger girl. The dark-haired girl had latched on to Janie like a lifeline, and Hank didn't have the heart to break the pair apart. But as Janie caught his eye, she broke away from her new friend and rushed to his side. "Dad, you should be Gemma's partner!"

"Janie—" His protest fell on deaf ears as his daughter continued.

"You heard what the guide said. Everyone needs a buddy. Besides—" Janie added, shooting him a look of reproach that was 100 percent Anne "—aren't you the one who said city girls and nature don't mix?"

Yeah, he'd said that all right. Because when it came to Gemma Chapman, it was easier to focus on their differences than on that instant attraction he'd felt the day before. A potential spark that he'd no doubt blown. But that was just as well. A city girl like her with a cowboy like him?

That was the combination that didn't mix.

When Janie first mentioned the nature hike, Gemma had imagined a short walk around the manor's sculpted grounds. Instead their guide took them on a trail away from Maverick Manor. Within mere minutes they had left the hotel and—as far as Gemma could tell—civilization behind. The farther they walked into the untamed land, the more uncertain she felt about…everything.

Including her footwear, she realized, as her heel hit a loose rock.

Gemma's leather ankle boots might have been made for walking the sidewalks of New York, but after twenty minutes, she had to admit they weren't fashioned for hiking the Montana wilderness.

Wasn't she supposed to be feeling at one with her surroundings? Experiencing some connection with the land? So far the only connection she'd made was with a low-hanging pine branch that had slapped her in the face when she'd been focused more on the path beneath her feet than the trail up ahead.

"You okay back there?"

Gritting her teeth, Gemma glared at Hank's broad back. She had no intention of admitting any of her concerns to the cocky, confident cowboy walking a few yards in front of her.

"Just peachy," she called out.

Truthfully, though, the trails leading from Maverick Manor were awe-inspiring. Evergreens rose on either side of the narrow dirt path and snowcapped granite peaks towered in the distance. But for a woman who lived her life surrounded by glass-and-chrome skyscrapers, Gemma found the Big Sky of Montana surprisingly claustrophobic, as nature seemed to be closing in on every side. Each time she heard a rustle in the underbrush or in the branches overhead, she cringed, thinking of the guide's warning to maintain a safe distance from any wildlife.

Safe distance. Gemma snorted. Right, because what was she going to do if she came across a bear? Run up and poke it with a stick? Who actually needed a warning like that?

You'll hate it, her mother had predicted when Gemma told her of her plan to go to Montana for her honeymoon. *You won't want to stay in the middle of nowhere for two days, let alone two weeks.*

Gemma didn't want to believe her mother was right.

Not about Montana, and not about the honeymoon. Not about the stories—the lies?—she'd told about Gemma's father.

"You don't have to do this, you know." Hank slowed his steps until she drew up alongside him. Janie and the rest of the kids, along with the hotel guide, had left them in the dust. Or more precisely in the mud, as the summer rains had made hiking the trails a watery version of hopscotch as she tried jumping over the puddles along the way.

He didn't seem to have any trouble navigating the path, looking completely at ease. His faded jeans hugged his long legs and the Western-style shirt he wore made his eyes look as blue as the skies overhead. He fit in so perfectly here, whereas she…

"If you want to go back—"

"I'm not going back to New York. Not yet."

Hank frowned. "Who said anything about New York? I meant the hotel."

"Oh." Gemma shook her head. "We can't do that. You heard what Janie said. The hotel wanted extra chaperones to make sure none of the kids fell behind."

Of course, with as far ahead as the kids were, there was no chance they would fall behind Hank and Gemma. He had been the one to volunteer the two of them to bring up the rear, no doubt expecting the city girl to fail miserably at Nature Walk 101.

Or maybe he was just trying to make things easier on you, a rational voice suggested. But Gemma wasn't in the mood for rational.

"I have to do this," she muttered, the words ending on a gasp as her boot heel hit a particularly slimy patch of mud and slipped right out from under her.

She squeezed her eyes shut, bracing for a fall into the cold puddle. Instead she fell back against a warm, solid chest. Her stunned gasp froze in her throat as Hank's muscular arm wrapped around her rib cage, just below her breasts.

"You okay?" he murmured in her ear.

As she glanced over her shoulder, their eyes met, their

faces mere inches apart. All it would take was for either of them to give an inch, and their lips would meet. As it was, Gemma felt the brush of warm breath against her skin. Awareness skittered across her nerve endings, and a shiver raised goose bumps across her flesh. The woodsy scent of his aftershave was a perfect complement to the evergreens surrounding them, and she wanted nothing more than to breathe him in.

Almost too late, she remembered his "entertaining" comment and jerked out of his embrace before he could offer some kind of "I told you so." She nearly slipped again, and as she righted herself, she held out a hand as if warding him off. "I've got it. I'm fine."

An impassive look on his face, Hank raised both of those impressive arms in an innocent-man gesture as he took a step back.

Innocent... Ha!

There was nothing innocent about the way her body responded to his. All of which made her voice sharper than she intended when she said, "I don't need your help."

"No, of course not."

Her cheeks heating, Gemma started back up the trail.

Falling into step with her, he said, "I don't suppose you want to tell me why you *have* to do this."

No one had understood. Not her friends. Not Chad. Certainly not her mother. So why did she think Hank Harlow might be the one person who would? She gave an inelegant snort as she skirted around a large rock in the middle of the muddy path.

Yeah, right. Because he'd proved the night before how well he understood her.

"This was all part of my Rust Creek Falls experience. You know, right up there with seducing a stranger on my honeymoon."

Gemma had the pleasure of watching those sculpted cheekbones turn red. "You're not going to let me forget that, are you?"

"Not anytime soon." She tossed her ponytail over her shoulder, but a little too much of her focus was on the hair flip and not enough on her next step. Her heel hit a rock. Her ankle twisted, but instead of the loose rock giving way beneath her foot, the whole trail seemed to disappear. She barely had time to scream before she was suddenly sliding down the steep embankment.

Branches and brush slapped at her face, but the undergrowth wasn't sturdy enough to slow her descent. Digging in her expensive boot heels had no effect, and for a split second Gemma pictured herself catapulting right off the side of a mountain.

Instead she splashed down into a muddy stream no more than a foot deep, but filled with enough cold water to steal what little breath she had left in her lungs. Gemma barely managed more than a shallow inhalation when she heard a wild crashing coming from the trail above. She cringed, covering her head with her hands. Was half the mountain about to give way on top of her?

"Gemma!" Concern filled Hank's voice as he half hopped, half slid down the same unintentional path she'd taken. "Are you okay?"

Lowering her arms, she took stock of the situation. She was wet and cold and thoroughly embarrassed. "I'm fine."

As he stared down at her, Hank's lips started to curve in a smile he wasn't trying all too hard to hide. He braced his hands on his hips. "Well, talk about something I won't be forgetting anytime soon…"

Gemma wouldn't have thought her face could get any hotter, but as anger burned away her embarrassment, she figured flames were about to start shooting from her eyes. Of course Hank could come crashing down the side of a mountain without a single speck of dirt or mud anywhere beyond the soles of his boots. Of course he could stand there looking all spotless and smug.

"You were just waiting for this, weren't you?" she muttered. "'City girls and nature don't mix,'" she echoed, dropping her voice an octave.

"Well, you've certainly proved me wrong. You're mixed up in nature right up to your eyebrows."

Gemma tried to push to her feet only to slip back onto her butt with a soggy splat. Her hand fisted in the muck, mud oozing between her fingers, as Hank's deep chuckle sent a shiver down her spine. The rugged sound was enough to make her belly clench, and despite her feeling like a fool, she couldn't help noticing the flash of his perfect white teeth and the way his blue eyes crinkled at the corners.

Bad enough that he was laughing at her. Did he have to look so good doing it?

Without giving herself a chance to think, she drew back a fistful of mud and fired. But as Hank bent down to help her up, the mud she'd aimed at his broad chest hit him right in the face.

For a stunned second, neither of them moved as the black slime dripped from his stubbled jaw onto his shirt. Finally he straightened and slowly lifted a hand. He wiped the mud from his face, shaking it from his fingers to plop into the wet ground at his feet.

Gemma swallowed. "Okay, I totally didn't mean to do that."

Reaching into his back pocket, he pulled out a folded white handkerchief. Because of course a man like Hank Harlow would carry one. She was pretty sure his wasn't monogrammed or made from pure silk. Which was probably a good thing considering the black muck he was wiping from his handsome face.

"You accidentally threw mud at me?"

"No, I purposely threw the mud. I accidentally hit you in the face. I was aiming for your chest."

"You missed."

"You moved—"

Gemma didn't have a chance to finish her sentence before Hank moved again. This time, reaching out for her with retribution gleaming in his blue eyes. Gemma tried to scramble away with no better luck pulling herself out on the second try.

Hank, however, had no such trouble. Catching her by the upper arms, he lifted her out of the mud and smack up against that broad chest she'd been aiming for. And if Gemma thought her sudden descent down the mountain had sent her pulse skyrocketing, that was nothing compared to Hank's lifting her into his arms. She braced her damp hands against his shoulders, the solid strength obvious beneath the thin material of his shirt.

Gemma wasn't sure what he'd initially intended, but Hank froze the moment their bodies came into contact. Heat flared in his eyes as he searched her features, and with her breasts pressed to the solid wall of his chest, she sensed the subtle change in the cadence of his breathing. Her gaze dropped to his mouth, so close to her own, and she ran her tongue along her suddenly tingling lips.

"Tell me about Chad."

Gemma jerked away and took a few soggy steps backward. Talk about being doused with cold mud! Gemma didn't want to think about her former fiancé, let alone talk about…

"Wait… What do you know about Chad?"

Hank lifted a broad shoulder in a diffident shrug. "Not much. Just that the guy evidently likes champagne, oysters and chocolate-covered strawberries."

"Chocolate…" Gemma's jaw dropped as he recited the exact menu from last night's room service order. "How—"

"I also know the guy's a total idiot."

"Because he likes champagne and oysters?" She doubted the combination would appeal to a rancher like Hank. Not that she could blame him where the oysters were concerned. Slimy little things… No wonder Chad liked them.

"He's an idiot for leaving you to eat them in the honeymoon suite alone."

Gemma's lips twisted at that. Walking over to a nearby boulder, she sat and pulled off her boots to pour out a rush of muddy water. "Chad didn't leave me alone in the honeymoon suite last night, Hank. *You* did."

Hank flinched and ran a hand through his hair, grimacing again when he came across some mud splattered by his ear. "Yeah, and I'm an idiot, too. It's no excuse, but it's been over a decade since I've been out on a date. Getting ready last night, all I could think was that I was bound to make a fool of myself in front of a woman like you—just like I did."

And there it was. That unexpected candor that had drawn her to Hank just as much as his broad shoulders and rugged good looks. His raw honesty was far more revealing than the swim trunks he'd been wearing the day before, and every bit as appealing. It was also enough to defuse some of her anger and make her look at the situation from his side. Hadn't she made some assumptions of her own when Hank no showed? Hadn't she immediately pictured him out with another woman? Ditching her for someone else—someone sexier and more seductive—the way Chad had?

Even so… She stomped back into her boots with a little more force than necessary. "I can't believe you thought I was…*trawling* for a date on my honeymoon."

"Honestly, I don't know what I thought. My head was filled with all kinds of doubts and that was before I found out you were staying in the honeymoon suite. And then when I saw the dinner cart and the card—but I should have at least called to cancel."

"Yes, you should have," Gemma retorted as she pushed away from the rocky ledge. But in the face of his open-book admission, she had to confess, "It would have saved me from thinking you'd stood me up to go out with another woman."

Hank stared at her without speaking long enough for Gemma to feel even more uncomfortable. Considering her clothes were soaked and she was standing in a pair of muddy boots, that was saying something.

Feeling completely vulnerable, Gemma turned away, but Hank caught her by the arm. His grip was warm and firm even through the soaked material. She could have pulled away but stood still instead, held in place more by the tingles of pleasure radiating out from his touch than by the strength of his hand.

She didn't turn back to face him, though, which only allowed Hank to step close behind her. She could feel the heat from his body against her chilled back as he leaned down to confess in her ear, "There isn't a woman at Maverick Manor—hell, in the state of Montana—that I would want to have dinner with rather than you." The husky murmur, combined with the whisper of breath against her neck, sent a shiver down her spine that had nothing to do with the cold water seeping through her clothes.

And oh, how her feminine pride and wounded ego wanted to believe him!

Pulling away before she melted right at his feet, she turned and asked, "Not even Janie?"

Hank smiled, but the intensity in his gaze never wavered as he said, "Janie doesn't count. She's a girl, not a woman."

And no doubt about it, Gemma Chapman was all woman.

Hank was all too aware of that fact—even before she lifted a slender hand to the silver tab at the center of her chest and unzipped the jacket she was wearing. His jaw dropped just as fast at the thin white tank top and luscious curves that were suddenly revealed.

"Uh, what are you doing?"

"This jacket is soaked," she said even as she peeled the wet material from her arms and did her best to wring out the water.

"Yeah, well, so are your pants."

She shot him a wry smirk at that. "Don't get your hopes up, cowboy." She knotted the sleeves of the jacket around her waist with a sharp tug. "I'm keeping them on."

As she set her hands on her hips, Hank had to drag his gaze from the swell of her breasts beneath the tank top's scooped neckline. Thank goodness her jacket had taken the brunt of her fall in the creek. Just the idea of Gemma in some kind of wilderness wet T-shirt contest was enough to have him breaking out in a sweat.

"So, how do we get back up there?" she asked as she looked up at the steep incline leading back to the trail.

"Same way we came down...only a lot slower." Taking the lead, Hank climbed up a few steps. He wedged his feet into the damp earth before he held out a hand. "Come on. You can do this."

Gemma sucked in a deep breath as she put her hand in his, and they started to make their way to the footpath above. He was right. The going was slow, and she slipped more than a few times, the air escaping from her lungs in a gasp and her fingers clenching around his wrist. When he asked if she wanted to stop for a break, she waved him off.

She was determined—he'd give her that—though completely out of her element. City girl through and through with her expensive workout clothes and ridiculous excuse for boots.

"Like you said…we can do this."

Actually, he'd said that *she* could do it. Hank hadn't felt the need to include himself in the reassurance. He'd walked farther distances and climbed steeper hills—often in knee-deep snow or with an injured calf over his shoulders.

But even so, there was something about the sound of that word that he liked. A long time had passed since his name had been linked with a woman's—and never with a woman like Gemma Chapman.

She was tougher than she looked, but more vulnerable, too.

Her beauty made it hard for him to believe she would ever have any doubt about her appeal, but her worry, even if only for a moment, that he had stood her up for another woman revealed an unexpected insecurity.

A triumphant grin lifted her lips as she climbed the final step back onto the path. A slight flush colored her cheeks and a few tendrils had slipped from her tidy ponytail to frame her face. "Yes! Success!"

Hank might have thought she'd just scaled Granite

Peak by her exuberant fist pump, and he wasn't about to ruin her moment. He figured any woman going on a honeymoon alone deserved something to celebrate.

Laughter drifted through the trees, and he guessed they had less than a minute before the kids and the Maverick Manor guide circled back their way. He caught Gemma's arm as she turned toward the sound. She glanced back, a question in her green eyes. The feel of her soft skin beneath his hand short-circuited his brain long enough for his unguarded expression to give her some kind of answer judging by the sudden, swift breath she took.

"I am sorry about last night," he finally managed to say, "but I meant what I said. There isn't another woman I want to go out with."

"In all of Montana," Gemma murmured.

"What?"

"You said there isn't another woman in all of Montana you want to go out with."

"That's right."

A faint hint of pink touched her cheeks, and she met his gaze with a challenging lift to her eyebrows. "You do realize Montana is one of the least populated states."

"You don't make things easy on a guy, do you?"

Her mouth twisted in a wry smile. "I think I've made things way too easy on guys in the past."

Guys like the fool in New York who had let her walk away.

"There's something you should know about real cowboys," he told her. "We aren't afraid of hard work. Let me prove that by making last night up to you."

"How?"

"By showing you a bit of real life in Rust Creek Falls."

Chapter Four

"I don't think I've ever been in a store where you can buy groceries, clothes and garden supplies all in one trip," Gemma said the following morning as she gazed around Crawford's General Store.

The redbrick building did indeed carry all those goods and more, and just like that, Hank's brilliant idea suddenly seemed like the stupidest one ever. His daughter's fascination with Gemma's wardrobe, along with her comment about him being a real cowboy, had given Hank the idea to take Gemma shopping for some genuine Western wear before they went riding. But unlike his suddenly fashion-conscious daughter, Hank didn't know designer labels from the ones his mom used to sew into his clothes when he was a kid.

He should have taken her into Kalispell, where they at least had a mall. The jeans and button-down shirts would all be off-the-rack and nothing fancy, but at least there they wouldn't be stockpiled at the end of an aisle containing oversize bags of dog food on one side and an assortment of leather work gloves on the other.

"Hey, Hank!" An excited female voice called out. "Can I help you find something?"

Hank swore beneath his breath. *Something else the Kalispell stores wouldn't have*, he thought to himself as he turned and met the wide-eyed, not-so-innocent stare of Natalie Crawford. The youngest Crawford, Natalie, along with her older sister, Nina, frequently worked at the family store.

Unlike Nina, who was happily married to Dallas Traub and raising a handful of kids, Natalie was still single and something of a flirt. Not that Hank ever took her seriously. No one took Natalie seriously. Everyone in town knew she had a penchant for causing trouble and seeking attention. With her big blue eyes, blond hair and curvy figure, she had a way of attracting both.

Normally Hank took the way she liked to give him a hard time as part of the service provided by Crawford's. But today he really, really wished Nina had been the one manning the aisles.

"I think we're good, Nat," he told her, not that she listened.

"Yeah, seems to me like you've got your hands full already," she mused, wiggling her eyebrows suggestively.

"Um, hi." Holding out her hand with a friendly smile, Gemma introduced herself. "I'm here on vacation and wanted to do some shopping while I'm in town."

"Well, I can tell you right now, you're not gonna find anything like that—" Natalie gave a wave at Gemma's sheer blouse and black leggings "—in Rust Creek Falls."

"I'm actually looking for something that would help me blend in a little."

Hank didn't think that was possible. Or necessary.

What he'd seen of her wardrobe so far was very Gemma—sexy, sophisticated and very big city. But he couldn't expect her to go riding without something far more casual to wear.

Natalie gave a small snort. "Why blend in when you can stand out? And around here, you will definitely stand out."

"We're going riding, Nat, so Gemma needs some boots, a pair of jeans and some kind of shirt." Turning to Gemma, he said, "I don't figure we'll be out too late, but if you start to get cold, you can always borrow my jacket."

"Aw, isn't that sweet?" Natalie interjected. "Giving Gemma your jacket... I think that means you're goin' steady."

Before Hank could protest, though he had no idea what he might say to discourage Natalie, the blonde started grabbing items off the shelves and shoving them into a startled Gemma's arms. "But you're not just going riding, right? I mean, Rust Creek Falls doesn't have much nightlife, but you'll want to have dinner at Maverick Manor, maybe shoot some pool over at the Ace in the Hole."

"I've never played pool before," Gemma confessed, as if admitting some deep, dark secret.

"Seriously? I thought big-city girls had all the experience, right, Hank?" Natalie flashed a wink at him before holding up a shirt and eyeballing Gemma. She added it to the growing pile in Gemma's arms and told her, "But hey, if you have a free night, let me know. I can show you some tricks, and we'll have a blast."

Hank did not want to be thinking about Gemma's experience or Natalie's tricks. He rubbed a sudden ache growing between his eyebrows. Why the hell hadn't he taken Gemma to the mall in Kalispell? "Neither of you should be going to the Ace in the Hole on your own," he insisted.

Single guys would be tripping all over themselves watching the beautiful blonde and the gorgeous brunette leaning over the green-felt table and lining up shots. He could just imagine some rowdy cowboy offering to help. Pressing up against Gemma, his arms around hers as he guided her hands along the pool stick...

Hank roughly reined in his imagination as the temperature in Crawford's General Store jumped about a hundred degrees.

"Oh, please, Hank! I already have four big brothers. Last thing I need is another one," Natalie argued. "What about you, Gemma?"

"Um, no brothers to speak of—big or otherwise. I'm an only child."

Natalie sighed. "Must be nice. All the attention, not to mention all the bathrooms to yourself."

"Growing up wasn't like that. At least not for me. I spent most of my childhood at a boarding school."

Hank's gut clenched as he tried to imagine sending Janie away for school and then clenched again as Gemma offered a smile that didn't reach her eyes. As she lowered her lashes, Hank caught a glimpse of the girl she'd been—all big green eyes, long dark hair, skinny arms and legs, dressed in some ubiquitous plaid uniform—lonely and lost and far from her family.

But then she gave her hair a quick toss, as if shaking off the momentary vulnerability, and joked, "So I spent my days sharing the bathroom with dozens of girls."

Natalie shuddered. "Worst nightmare ever! You have my complete sympathy. In fact—" she said as she slid Hank a not-so-subtle grin "—we should commiserate over a beer or two at the Ace in the Hole before you leave."

"Well, we were supposed to go there the other night but…something came up," Gemma finished but not before sliding a reproachful look his way, over the growing mound of clothing.

Okay, so not out of the doghouse yet. Well, he had told her he wasn't afraid of hard work, and Gemma deserved to know she was worth the effort. But as Natalie glanced at him with a curious expression on her face, Hank felt the need to explain, "Janie had a headache."

Natalie huffed out a sound as she went back to digging through the clothes like his dad's old retriever burrowing through his mom's vegetable garden. "At least it was Janie with the headache. Because when a woman gives a guy that excuse, it usually means… Well…" She stopped to give him a once-over over her shoulder. "I can't imagine too many women round here giving you that kind of a brush-off, Hank."

"Yeah, well, as it was pointed out to me recently, Montana is one of the least populated states."

"Huh?"

He thought he heard Gemma give a small laugh, but he couldn't tell for sure now that she was practically hidden by a pile of clothes that would last her for the next two years, forget the next week.

"Never mind, and I think we're good, Nat…unless you're hoping we're going to buy out all of Crawford's inventory."

The blonde heaved a sigh that reminded Hank of his daughter, as well as the "you don't know anything" eye roll to go with it. "No, I don't expect Gemma to buy all this. First she has to try the clothes on."

"Seriously?" He'd been shopping at Crawford's for years. "You have a dressing room?"

"Of course we have a dressing room! How else would our customers be able to buy clothes?"

"Um, by size?"

This time Natalie wasn't the only female giving an exasperated sigh. "Men," Natalie said with a conspirator's glance at Gemma. She grabbed his arm as she walked by. "Come on. Dressing rooms are back this way."

As he found himself dragged down a hallway toward the employees-only area, Hank realized why he'd never spotted the rooms before. Natalie pushed aside a striped curtain and revealed a cubicle small enough that he would have banged both elbows had he ever felt the need to try a shirt on before buying it. A full-length mirror, a small bench and a single hook were the only amenities inside.

He half expected Gemma to turn up her nose at the space, but as she dumped the load of clothes onto the bench, a big smile lit her face. Holding up a sleeveless black-and-red checkered shirt against her torso, she grinned at him as their gazes met in the mirror. "What do you think? Does this say Montana cowgirl or is it too Pacific Northwest lumberjack?"

Realizing Gemma was about to take her clothes off, Hank's thoughts stalled there, and he couldn't quite get his mind to move forward fast enough to comment on what she'd be putting on instead. "Uh—"

Fortunately Natalie jumped in and said, "Try it on, and we'll see." After sliding the curtain closed with a flick of her wrist, she turned to face him with a smug smile. "'Bout time you got back in the saddle," she murmured beneath her breath.

"I'm a rancher, Nat," Hank deadpanned. "I'm in the saddle a good ten to twelve hours a day."

"Not what I meant, and you know it," she said in a singsong voice.

Hank did know it. He also knew he felt far more than a little uncomfortable standing right outside the dressing room. With the full-length curtain pulled closed, he couldn't see anything. But he didn't need to see to imagine Gemma sliding those leggings down her long, slender legs, pulling the loose blouse over her head and letting her long dark hair tumble over her bare shoulders and back... And he could hear the rustle of clothing that made everything he was picturing less like imagination and more like a reality that was one whisk of a curtain away.

He practically jumped when the jingling rings sailed across the metal rod.

"What do you think?"

Holy...

Hank didn't know what he'd expected to see when Gemma pulled back that curtain. After all, at their first meeting she'd been wearing less material than it took to make a handkerchief. He knew how gorgeous she was. Sexy, sophisticated, big-city chic. Everything about that woman had exuded *look but don't touch.* But this...

Skintight indigo denim hugged her long legs, skimming over every curve in a way that had his palms tingling to do the same. As his hungry gaze moved upward, he took in the sleeveless blouse she'd chosen. Not the checkered one she'd held up earlier, but a red bandanna print that showed off the toned muscles and smooth skin of her arms. And maybe there was something to be said for paying the big bucks for designer outfits because the maker of this shirt had clearly cut corners when it came to adding buttons. The material gaped in the center of her chest, revealing a hint of black lace along with the soft swell of her breasts.

This was girl next door...all grown up.

And all the reasons why Hank had told himself to keep his distance—the differences in their lives, in their locations, in his reluctance to risk his heart in any kind of relationship—seemed to have been brushed aside with one magical swipe of a dressing-room curtain.

"Hank?" Gemma tilted her head as she looked at him, and he realized she'd pulled her hair up into a ponytail, adding to the country-girl image. It was all he could do to stay where he was and not rush inside to test if that tiny dressing room was big enough for something other than bumping elbows.

"I, uh..."

"I think you've shocked him speechless," Natalie said gleefully, "though with these strong, silent types, it's hard to tell."

A distant bell rang, and the blonde excused herself with a roll of her eyes. "I better go see who that is, but don't try on any more outfits without letting me see!"

Hank wasn't sure his heart—or his suddenly raging libido—could take another wardrobe reveal. As Gemma turned back to the mirror, he could see her expression reflected back at him over her shoulder. If he'd been struck speechless when Gemma pulled back the curtain, she looked—hell, Gemma looked like her fairy godmother had just waved a magic wand and made all her wardrobe wishes come true. As she brushed her hands across the denim and carefully adjusted the pointed collar, she didn't seem to notice she wasn't draped in a glittering ball gown.

"It's perfect, isn't it?" she asked, her eyes shimmering so brightly that Hank might have thought she was on the verge of tears if not for the huge smile on her face.

He gave his head a quick shake. He knew a woman like Gemma would get into shopping, but this...

"It looks just like…"

"Like what?" he asked when her voice trailed off.

"Like something a real cowgirl would wear," she whispered. "Doesn't it?"

"It does," he agreed, his voice sounding rough and raw, and Hank had to remind himself that it was all an illusion. Even in the wilds of Montana, he had come across enough "cowboys" who were all hat and no horses. Clothes did not necessarily make the man. Or woman, in this case.

Just because Gemma suddenly looked like she could fit right in at Rust Creek Falls, that didn't change who she was. A city girl with a career and a life waiting for her back in New York City. Not to mention a former fiancé. Hank still didn't know why Gemma had called off the wedding. But he'd already fooled himself once into thinking he could hold on to a woman who'd never truly been his. It was a mistake his heart couldn't handle him making again.

Gemma didn't know when she first heard the expression *you can't miss what you've never had*. All she knew was that it wasn't true.

Not when what she was missing was the father she'd never known.

She knew it was completely ridiculous to get so emotional, and maybe her mother was right. Maybe this was all just a game of dress up. But wearing an outfit so similar to the one in the picture of herself as a toddler, Gemma didn't feel like she was pretending to be someone else. Instead she felt as though she were seeing the person she might have been…had life turned out differently.

Had her father not been killed in a car accident only a few months after that photo was taken.

As a child, she'd asked about her father, but all her mother would say was that he had left them when he discovered Diane was pregnant. Gemma had no reason to believe otherwise until she'd gone looking for something old and found a forgotten box in her mother's closet. A box that contained not just a single picture of her in toddler Western wear but dozens. And unlike the photograph of herself as a child, one where she'd been alone in the shot, many of these pictures showed her in the arms of a handsome, smiling cowboy.

Her father.

Her father might have left when her mother got pregnant, but Diane was the one who'd skipped out on the part of the story where he came back. And not just once or twice. Judging from the timeline of the photos, he'd returned on multiple occasions, from when Gemma was a few months old, right up until that fateful car crash weeks before her fourth birthday.

Gemma only knew the date because in that same box was a copy of her father's death certificate. On that form, she'd discovered his birthplace, a tiny town called Rust Creek Falls.

Despite her high-paying job, despite her trendy apartment, despite her envy-inspiring wardrobe, despite her engagement to Chad, Gemma had always felt the hole in her heart. And maybe this trip was a wild-goose chase. Or maybe it was her one chance to discover some kind of connection to the man—and to the girl—in those photographs.

She couldn't expect Hank to understand, but if he thought she was crazy, he hid it well. Much better, she realized with a sudden swallow, than the desire burning hot in his gorgeous eyes.

Stripping off her New York wardrobe, she'd been all too aware of Hank standing outside the small dressing room. Not that it was much of a room. More like a cubicle with a curtain. A thin wisp of material that had done little to block Gemma's thoughts of the rugged rancher on the other side.

"It does look like something a real cowgirl would wear," he agreed, and was it her imagination or did his voice sound a little huskier than a few moments ago? He lifted a hand, and her heart skipped a beat. "Except for these."

He trailed his fingers along her silver chandelier-style earrings, and a shiver raced down her spine as his knuckles brushed against the side of her neck.

"A cowgirl can still accessorize, can't she?"

"Sure she can." He snatched his hand back, and his expression turned remote as if the sensual moment had never happened. "If she's a New York City cowgirl."

The reminder that Gemma didn't belong had her stepping back into the dressing room. "Can you let Natalie know I'm buying the outfit?"

"Which one?"

Offering a cheeky smile, she said, "All of them," before swiping the dressing-room curtain right in front of his face.

Gemma had enough clothes back in New York to know retail therapy could easily fill a closet while doing little to fill the hole in her heart. But she still bought enough clothes to overload several shopping bags. The final touch was the one she loved most—a genuine pair of tooled boots in a butter-soft, honey-brown leather.

Though she had plenty of boots in her shoe collection—and with as many pairs as she owned, it was impossible not to consider it a collection—something about the cowboy boots made her feel different.

Not necessarily taller, since many of her boots back home had much higher stiletto points. But something about the solid chunky heels beneath her feet gave her an added level of confidence. Like she could take on horse-back riding or steer wrangling or whatever cowgirls did. Including the challenge of facing down the stubborn cowboy in front of her.

"Absolutely not," Gemma stated as Hank reached for his wallet. "You are not paying for my clothes."

Having booked the honeymoon suite herself, she knew a stay at Maverick Manor was not cheap. Janie had remarked more than once about how hard her dad worked—often from sunup to sundown—and how this was his first vacation in years. She had the feeling the hotel stay was a stretch for the hardworking rancher's budget. She wasn't about to let his ego wear his wallet even thinner.

"A gentleman always pays," he insisted.

Standing behind the register, Natalie snorted at that, and Hank closed his eyes, his expression pained.

"It was my idea to come here," he continued.

"And my idea to go riding. So how much will I owe you for that?" Gemma asked, reaching into her purse and pulling out a credit card of her own with a lift to her eyebrows.

"Yeah, Hank," Natalie chimed in, watching their exchange with so much interest that Gemma half expected the woman to break out a box of popcorn for the afternoon's entertainment. "How much do you charge for a ride? And is that by the hour or...?"

Swearing beneath his breath, Hank seemed to get that he was outnumbered. "Fine."

"Fine," Gemma countered.

Natalie plucked the card from Gemma's fingers and rang up her purchase. "Okay, so, first fight. Now y'all get to kiss and make up."

They didn't kiss, but at the mention, Gemma swore Hank's gaze dropped to her suddenly tingling lips. Her breath caught in her chest, and only a not-so-subtle throat clearing from Natalie reminded Gemma that she needed to sign the sales receipt. After scribbling her name at the bottom of the slip, she started to reach for the shopping bags, but Hank stilled her with a glance.

And okay…she didn't mind a guy carrying her purchases, so long as she was the one to pay for them.

Hank was silent as they left the general store, and Gemma hoped she hadn't offended his masculine pride. "Look, if you're worried about what it's costing me to stay in the honeymoon suite, don't be. Everything at Maverick Manor—and I do mean everything—is getting charged to my former fiancé's account."

If she thought that announcement would ease Hank's mind, the scowl on the rancher's handsome face quickly proved otherwise. Though the mountains in the distance standing like sentinels over the town were too far away to provide an actual echo, Gemma cringed as she heard her own words bounce back at her.

Her friends, those who hadn't tried talking her out of the honeymoon for one, had encouraged her to stick it to Chad's wallet, the same way he'd been sticking it to Melanie Williamson. Hell hath no fury, and all of that.

Gemma had insisted she wasn't out for revenge—that she was simply making the best of a bad situation. So why did she have to open her mouth and say something that made her sound so petty and spiteful?

She was still trying to figure out how to get her foot, boot and all, out of her mouth when they reached Hank's truck. He unlocked the passenger-side door and placed her bags inside. "Wait here. There's something I need to get."

"I can go with you," she offered, but he was already shaking his head.

"I'll be right back."

Bemused, Gemma watched as he headed back toward Crawford's. She used the time to study the sights, turning her attention away from Hank's broad shoulders and faded-to-perfection jeans only once he disappeared inside the store. Main Street ran through the center of the town. Standing on the corner, Gemma could see a lovely stone church, complete with a soaring steeple and stone steps leading toward the arched doorway. The perfect backdrop for a bride and groom as they rushed toward a waiting car while guests tossed birdseed and wishes for a bright and beautiful future.

She and Chad had agreed to forgo a church wedding, planning the ceremony and reception at a five-star hotel, and she was suddenly glad. She could look at the church, imagining those happy newlyweds, untainted by memories of the wedding that wasn't.

She offered a polite smile as an older woman walked down the sidewalk toward the store. "Good morning."

Instead of responding to the greeting and heading inside, the woman stopped short. She stared at Gemma with her faded eyes narrowing behind her glasses before finally shaking her gray head. "I'm sorry, dear. I'm afraid I don't remember your name."

"Oh." Gemma gave a small laugh at what could only be a case of mistaken identity. "It's Gemma Chapman, but we've never met."

"Gemma Chapman," the woman mused as the bell above the door rang and Hank stepped outside, a good-sized paper bag in hand.

"Morning, Melba," he greeted the older woman. "I see you've met Gemma. Gemma, this is Melba Strickland. She and her husband, Gene, run the boardinghouse in town."

Still gazing at Gemma, the older woman barely seemed to hear Hank. "Gemma Chapman," she repeated once more. "No, that's not right."

Hank's brow rose. "I'm pretty sure Gemma knows her own name."

Melba straightened to her full height. "Don't be smart, young man," she warned, causing both Hank and Gemma to try to hide their smiles as they exchanged a glance. "I have a remarkable memory, and I've seen you before, young lady. I'm sure of it."

Gemma lifted a questioning shoulder. "I'm afraid I only arrived in Rust Creek Falls on Saturday, and unless you've ever been to New York..." When Melba snorted at the idea, Gemma suggested, "Then I guess I must just have one of those faces."

This time it was Hank's turn to snort.

Her eyes still narrowed in concentration, Melba shook her head. "Give me time. It'll come to me."

As they watched Melba shuffle off into the store, Hank said, "The Stricklands have been running their boarding-house for decades. I can't imagine the number of people who've passed through those doors."

"I must have reminded her of a past boarder." But it was strange that the longtime Rust Creek Falls resident hadn't seen her as someone new to the town but instead as someone who'd been there before. Perhaps even as someone who belonged.

Gesturing to the bag in Hank's hand, she asked, "Did you get what you need?"

Hank held her gaze as he reached inside. "I got what *you* need."

"Hank..." She started to protest as he pulled out a cowboy hat. A straw cowboy hat, complete with a braided pink hatband. Her words disappeared with a quick gasp as he placed it on her head,

"Even a wannabe cowgirl can't go riding without a hat."

"Oh..." Desperately wishing for a mirror, she used

the next best thing, turning toward Crawford's front window, where she could make out a faint image reflected back at her. Like finding that long-ago picture, Gemma barely recognized herself. She certainly didn't look like the stressed-out New York executive who'd been working around the clock just to get time off for her honeymoon. Nor did she look like the humiliated and betrayed former fiancée who'd arrived in Rust Creek Falls.

No, this was someone new: the little girl in the picture who'd finally had a chance to grow up into the woman she was always meant to be.

Unexpected tears flooded her eyes. "Hank, it's…it's perfect."

His expression half quizzical, half alarmed, he murmured, "Man, you really do like clothes, don't you?"

Unable to explain her emotional reaction, Gemma gave a watery laugh. "You have no idea."

The red bandanna-print shirt and denim jeans were so much more than clothes; they were a tangible connection to the past and the father she'd never known. For all she knew, he might have bought the outfit she'd worn in that thirty-year-old picture along this very street. Maybe even at that very same store.

But the hat…

The hat was part of her present. From the good-looking cowboy who'd given her a gift greater than he could imagine.

"Oh, my gosh!" Janie exclaimed. "I love this!"

Gemma grinned at the young girl's enthusiasm. She and Hank had met up with Janie after their trip to Crawford's. Janie had filled them in on the scavenger hunt the kids had done on the hotel grounds—capturing images of items with their cell phones to win the game. Hank had shaken his head a bit at the added use of technology to the old-fashioned game, but he patiently listened to his daughter as she went through all of the pictures.

After that, she'd asked to go to Gemma's room to see the clothes she'd bought. Hank—likely already worn-out and bored from too much shopping—had immediately passed on the idea. Which was just as well, considering what should have been a quick reveal of the jeans and shirts Gemma had purchased had turned into a full-on fashion show.

Only with Janie modeling Gemma's New York wardrobe.

Janie spun in a circle, Gemma's tunic-style geometric-print blouse fitting the girl like an oversize dress. Not that Janie seemed to care. She wobbled in the too-big heels as she turned to Gemma with a huge smile. "You have the coolest clothes ever!"

Despite Janie's fervent vow and her fascination with clothes and jewelry, Gemma couldn't help but notice the young girl's own style was decidedly tomboy. Along with her denim and flannel shirts, her blond hair was simply tucked behind her ears, her face free of even a hint of lip gloss. The preteen would look adorable in something, well, a little less cowgirl.

"Do you have any shirts like that one?" Gemma asked her.

"Are you kidding? All I have are T-shirts with cartoon characters on them. And you should see the dress my mom bought me for Easter." Janie's exasperated expression told the story even before she added, "It's the same dress I had, like, three years ago! When I was in third grade! I just finished sixth grade. I'm practically a teenager! Sometimes we go to the mall in Kalispell, but it's like they have *too much* stuff, and it'd probably all look stupid on me anyway," she finished with a self-conscious shrug.

"Hey, you would not look stupid." Gemma firmly turned Janie toward the mirror and met the girl's eyes in the reflection. "You would look amazing in an outfit just like that one…but maybe we could find one a little closer to your size."

Janie giggled at that, and Gemma gave a relieved sigh. Preteen crisis averted.

Too bad she'd made such a stink about paying for her own clothes. She and Janie would have a total blast hitting every junior section in the mall. Of course Hank had bought her the hat, but still… She didn't want to overstep when it came to his daughter, or when it came to his pride.

But maybe there was something girlie she and Janie could do.

"So, you and my dad are going riding tomorrow, huh?" Janie's eyes gleamed. "You must be so excited!"

Gemma wasn't sure *excited* was the word. Now that horseback riding was no longer something that might happen someday and was instead happening the very next day, anticipation was quickly turning into trepidation.

"Are you sure you don't want to come with us?" Maybe seeing that riding a horse was something a child could do would help calm her nerves. But Janie was already shaking her head.

"Some of the kids are going on a fishing trip down by the creek. Besides," she added with a hopeful look, "this way you and my dad can be alone. I know he really likes you."

"Do you think so?" Gemma cringed at the eager sound of her own voice. Good grief! Which one of them was the adolescent girl?

Janie nodded. "I can tell. It's like when my best friend Abby's mom met Autry Jones. Abby just knew they would fall in love and get married. Now they're all living in Paris."

"Oh, wow!" Stunned by that whirlwind explanation of a relationship and fearing what Janie might have in mind for her and Hank, Gemma said, "I, um... I'm not sure how your dad would like being a rancher in Paris."

"He's not gonna go to Paris, silly!" Some of Janie's excitement dimmed as the logistical reality of Gemma's living in New York seemed to sink in. She hopped up from the bed, stumbling a bit in Gemma's heels. "I just want him to be happy, you know? A few years ago, Homer Gilmore spiked the punch at a wedding, and after that a bunch of people got married. So I thought about seeing if he could put something in my dad's coffee. But I'm not real sure where Mr. Gilmore lives, and he's kinda scary."

"Janie!"

"Then two years ago, Zach Dalton took out an ad in the newspaper for a wife, so I thought that's what I should do for my dad."

Taking out a newspaper ad for a wife? Gemma might not have known Hank for very long, but she had no doubt the somewhat-stoic rancher would be mortified. But even worse was the thought of Janie seeking out some strange, kinda-scary old man to put some unknown substance in her father's morning cup of joe!

Leaning forward to meet the girl's gaze, Gemma said, "Promise me you won't contact the newspaper or Mr. Gilmore."

"I won't have to." Completely ignoring the dire warning in Gemma's voice, the young girl beamed at her. "Because you're here!"

Chapter Five

Hank couldn't have picked a more beautiful morning for riding. The summer day was warm but with enough clouds in the big blue Montana sky to offer a break from the beaming sun. A cool breeze sifted through the trees and green grasses, carrying the scent of pine and clean mountain air. And Gemma was just as fresh and beautiful and breathtaking as the land he loved.

They'd talked on the drive over, though Hank couldn't have said about what. He'd been too busy trying to keep his eyes on the road and his hands on the wheel instead of letting them roam all over the woman in the passenger seat. She was wearing one of the outfits from her shopping spree at Crawford's the day before, though not the one that had brought tears to her eyes and nearly brought him to his knees.

She'd wanted to ride with the window down, unconcerned by the way the wind was whipping through her ponytail. The faded denim jeans fit her like a glove, and the pink-and-white checkered Western shirt had enough pearl snaps to keep her covered and to keep him sane. He was glad to see she'd changed out her dangling earrings for a sparkling pair of diamond studs. The likelihood of the jewelry getting caught on something was small, but this was Gemma's first ride, and he would do everything to keep her safe.

As they rounded a curve in the road, Hank spotted a familiar horse trailer parked along a turnout to one of the many hiking trails around Rust Creek Falls. He'd asked one of his hands, Russell Neal, to load up two of his best horses, and the younger man stood holding the reins of the already saddled rides.

"Hey, boss." The young hand grinned as he handed over the reins, freeing up his right hand to tip his hat toward Gemma. "Ma'am."

"Ma'am…" Gemma imitated Russell's deep drawl and then gave a laugh. "You cowboys and your manners." Holding out her hand, she said, "I'm Gemma Chapman."

Russell quirked a grin as his large hand engulfed her small, delicate one. "Ma'am," he repeated to Gemma's delight.

Hank gritted his teeth at his employee's obvious flirting. In his early twenties, Russell was still sowing his oats, picking up part-time work on ranches while trying to find fame and fortune on the rodeo circuit. The kid worked hard—Hank would give him that—but he was also a bit reckless and wild, out for excitement and adventure.

All of which made him too young for Gemma, and all of which made Hank wonder if he wasn't too old.

"Daylight's wasting," he said abruptly, putting a sudden end to Russell's down-home charm.

"Yessir." With a final tip of his hat to Gemma, Russell confirmed he'd be back to pick up the horses in a few hours. The truck rumbled off, the low-pitched hum and smell of diesel fading as the trailer rounded the bend in the highway.

He turned back to find Gemma studying him with a concerned gaze. The midmorning breeze picked up, sweeping her ponytail over one shoulder so the feathered ends rested against the curve of her breast. "Hank, are you sure about this?"

Not about one damn thing... And if there was anything he hated, it was not knowing where he stood. He'd felt that way through most of his marriage, once he realized that Anne was never getting over Dan Stockton and that her relationship—and the man himself—would never be part of the past.

And now here he was with Gemma. A woman unlike anyone he'd met before, fresh from what he assumed was a painful breakup, on a honeymoon for one with all of New York City waiting for her back home.

"It's just a horseback ride," he said as much to reassure himself as to smooth over whatever worries Gemma might harbor.

But as it turned out, her worries had traveled a very different path. "I know, but Russell had to take time out of his day to haul the horses out here, and it's not like you own a riding stable. I'm sure these horses have more important jobs than going on a pleasure ride. I don't want any of the other men to be shorthanded. Or...would that be short-hooved?"

"Short-*hooved*?" he echoed with a laugh he quickly smothered when he realized Gemma was serious.

Everyone in Rust Creek Falls knew Hank had turned the Bar H into one of the most successful ranches in the area, but of course Gemma wasn't from Rust Creek Falls. Even though Janie had gone on in embarrassing length about how successful he was, Gemma didn't seem to understand how many hands and hooves worked the ranch.

The big bay stallion, Hondo, was Hank's own horse, the one he rode for work and pleasure. And the palomino with the pale streak beneath its forelock… "This is Lightning," he said by way of introduction. "He belonged to my mother." The big gelding was too old for ranch work, but his mother had loved that horse. "He's retired now, but he'll always have a home at the Bar H."

"That's so sweet." Gemma's lovely features softened into a tender smile women usually reserved for cooing over chubby-cheeked babies and fluff-ball kittens.

"Yeah, that's me all right," he muttered, feeling like he'd heard that statement his whole life.

Nice-guy Hank Harlow.

"He's gorgeous, but are you sure you don't have a smaller horse I could ride? Maybe one pony-sized and possibly with training wheels?"

One corner of Hank's mouth hitched up in a half smile. "Lightning's just big-boned." He ran his hand down the side of the large horse's neck. "But he's also as steady as they come. You could set off firecrackers at his feet and he wouldn't move a hoof."

"Tell me we won't be putting that to the test today."

"Not a chance. Just letting you know you're safe with him." Hank might not know how to laugh and flirt like one of his ranch hands, but he knew horses and he knew how to protect the people around him. Checking on one of the straps holding the saddle in place, he gruffly added, "You're safe with me."

You're safe with me.

Gemma knew that. Down to her bones. Everything about Hank Harlow spoke of integrity and respect. She trusted him to keep her safe. That trust just hadn't transferred to the thousand-pound horse standing in front of her yet.

But part of her honeymoon for one was about taking chances and doing what she wanted to do. And riding a horse was something she wanted to do. In theory. The reality was a bit more daunting than she'd expected.

"You don't have to go through with this, you know," Hank told her.

"But you went to so much trouble…"

Gemma's voice trailed off as she realized how closely the words echoed the conversation she'd had when she told her mother about Chad's cheating. Only, Gemma had been the one to say she couldn't go through with the marriage, and her mother had pointed out all the trouble—and expense—she and Gemma's stepfather had gone through in paying for the wedding.

As if that was a bigger concern than exchanging vows to love, honor and cherish with a cheating louse who couldn't keep it in his pants in the days leading up to the ceremony!

But as Gregory Chapman's stepdaughter, Gemma had very much been about silently going with the flow and not making waves.

"No trouble," Hank insisted.

"But the horses…"

"It's no trouble," he repeated with the same infinite patience he showed when Janie had asked him at least a half dozen times in the span of fifteen minutes about all they had planned.

And just like he had said then, he added, "It's your vacation, Gem. Anything you want."

And oh, wasn't that a dangerous suggestion! His deep

voice murmuring the shortened version of her name and his offer of *anything* sent a shiver down her spine.

"I want to do this. I do." Trying to keep the butterflies at bay, she joked, "After all, I've got the outfit and the boots and everything."

Hank's lips tipped up at the corners at her adamant statement. "You had the bathing suit, too."

"What?"

"At the pool," he reminded her, "you had the bathing suit, but you never went in the water."

"I stuck my feet in," she argued. And she had. At the steps in the shallow end. Which suddenly seemed so pathetic. Was that what she really wanted? To spend her life in the shallow end? Afraid of taking chances, of making waves?

No. At least not anymore. If it was, then she would have married Chad. After all, she already had the dress and the heels and everything.

"Okay, let's do this." Sucking in a deep breath, she stepped toward the horse and reached for the handle-thingy on the saddle.

"Whoa, there, Annie Oakley." Hank caught her with a muscled arm around the waist before she could try to hike her way up onto the huge horse. His breath was warm and his voice amused as he murmured into her ear, "Buy a guy a drink first, would ya?"

"Oh, I, um, guess I was rushing things?"

"It's your first time, so you want to take things easy. And remember, we've got all day."

Okay, they were still talking about riding horses... weren't they? With his muscled arm wrapped around her waist, Gemma could think of a few other firsts. Like turning in his arms and feeling that first whisper of breath, that first brush of his lips against hers, that first taste of him on her tongue.

"You want to take a minute to get to know the horse first."

"Oh, right." So they really *were* still talking about horseback riding.

"Here." Taking her hand in his, he guided her palm along the horse's neck. The animal's coat was warm and bristly beneath her palm. When Lightning snorted and tossed his head with a jingle of the reins, Gemma would have jumped back, but with Hank standing behind her, she had nowhere to go.

"Easy," he murmured, and Gemma didn't know if he was talking to her or to the horse. She wasn't even sure it mattered, as her nerves had calmed. Lightning glanced at her with the biggest, darkest eyes she'd ever seen, a soulful sweetness shining out from the chocolate-brown depths.

She reached out again, this time without Hank to guide her. "Hey, sweetheart. Aren't you just a gorgeous guy?"

The horse nickered again, and this time Gemma laughed softly as the animal almost seemed to nod in agreement. "Of course you are. And you've already heard my deep, dark secret. Probably seems silly to you, doesn't it? That I've never ridden a horse before. I planned this whole Wild West vacation so I could do all the things I'd dreamed of doing, but—sometimes things don't work out the way you plan."

Though Gemma stood facing the horse with Hank at her back, she could sense his stillness. Because of course she hadn't simply planned a vacation. She'd planned a honeymoon. She'd planned a wedding. She'd planned to be married.

Nothing in her extensive plans had her standing in the arms of a Montana rancher.

Unwittingly, Gemma's hand paused along the horse's warm neck, and she started when the animal swung his large head toward her and nudged her arm.

Hank chuckled. "Lightning can be a bit pushy when it comes to what he wants."

"What does he want?" she asked as she glanced over her shoulder.

"What any guy wants," he murmured. "The attention of a beautiful woman."

They rode through rolling green hills and towering trees and along a sparkling stream on a mountain trail that Hank said would lead to the waterfall the town was named after. Gemma tried to enjoy the glorious scenery, but her entire attention was focused on staying in the saddle.

Despite Hank's patient instruction to loosen up her knees, relax her back and rock her hips in time with Lightning's rhythm, she felt more like she was bouncing on a pogo stick than riding a horse.

"You're doing great!" he encouraged as he rode next to her, so fluid and natural astride Hondo that he looked like he was born to it. And so effortlessly masculine and sexy that Gemma's mouth went dry. "You feeling okay?"

She might have nodded, but with the way her head was bobbing up and down along with the rest of her body, she figured Hank wouldn't even be able to tell. "Great," she said, her voice bouncing in time with her backside hitting the leather saddle.

Hank laughed. "Don't worry. It takes a while to find your seat."

Gemma didn't think she'd have any trouble finding her seat. She had a good idea that it would be black-and-blue, and the bruises there would certainly be making themselves known. She stared out over the beautiful landscape, but she couldn't quite swallow the lump of disappointment lodged in her throat. "I'm awful at this."

After only about fifteen minutes, Hank reined Hondo to a stop and Lightning immediately slowed as well. So that was it. Her great horseback-riding adventure was ending in failure. Maybe she'd built the whole thing up in her mind too much. Seen too many romantic movies with handsome cowboys and their bold, brave cowgirls riding across wide-open meadows. Perhaps if she'd learned as a child, the way Janie likely had, then things might have been different. But now it was too late to learn, too late to change.

Did she really think anything would be different when she went back home? Back to her high-rent apartment, back to her designer wardrobe, back to her sixty-hour workweeks. Or would she simply fall back into the same routine that should have made her happy and proud and fulfilled…and yet didn't?

Blinking back ridiculous tears, Gemma forced herself to meet Hank's gaze and braced herself for some "city girl" comment. Sure enough, he cocked one of his eyebrows the same way he had when he called her out on staying in the shallow end of the pool. "Quitting already?"

Her jaw dropped. "Me? You're the one who stopped. I figured you'd…given up on me."

The smile slid from his face as he dismounted. He kept Hondo's reins in one hand as he walked over to Lightning's side.

"What are you doing?" she asked as he slipped her boot from first one stirrup and then the other.

"Trying something new." And before she had any idea what he intended, he swung up into the saddle behind her. Gemma barely had time to gasp, as she was suddenly plastered up against Hank's solid body, her back to his chest, her thighs running alongside his, his arm bracketed low across her hips.

"And for the record," he murmured into her ear as he kicked the horse into motion, Hondo walking beside them, his reins in Hank's hands, "we're just getting started."

A half hour and what felt to Gemma like a hundred miles later, Hank pulled both horses to a stop at the sparkling falls. He swung down first and then reached back up to help her from the saddle. This time they ended up pressed chest to chest as she slid down Hank's body until her feet touched the ground.

"Easy there," he murmured as she stumbled, her legs suddenly feeling as weak as wet noodles. "I told you you'd get the hang of it."

Breathless and exhilarated and not sure how much of that had to do with the wild ride and how much was due to the rancher, she grinned up at him. "That was amazing! And this…"

The towering waterfall was breathtaking, spilling into the stone-lined pool below, the spray creating a brilliant rainbow. A stand of cottonwoods ringed the meadow, offering plenty of shady spots to rest and relax in the cool summer grass. "It's beautiful. Pictures don't do it justice."

"Pictures?"

Gemma nodded. "I went online and did some research before coming here. I read about Falls Mountain, Owl Rock." She laughed lightly. "I watched every episode of *The Great Roundup*."

"This is a great town, and for those of us who live here, it certainly has its charms. But it isn't the kind of place where someone would typically plan a honeymoon. There are dozens of places—bigger, far more popular— that would cross most people's minds long before anyone ever came across Rust Creek Falls. So why here?"

Keeping with the simplest answer, Gemma said, "Rust Creek Falls was my father's hometown. He was born here."

"Seriously?"

She nodded. "Yes. His name was Daryl Reems."

She waited with bated breath as Hank paused for a moment before he shook his head. "Don't recognize the name."

What had she expected after so many years? But she turned back to Lightning, so Hank wouldn't see the disappointment in her face. "Well, that would have been almost sixty years ago. And he moved around a lot during his life."

That was what Diane had always told her, and thanks to the box in her mother's closet, Gemma knew at least that much was true. Along with the photographs from her childhood, she found postcards her father had sent. Images of the Grand Canyon, Utah's national parks, a Hatch Chili Festival in New Mexico and Mount Rushmore. Dozens of places and rarely the same state more than twice. Thanks to the postmarks, she'd been able to trace his routes over the first three and a half years of her life, including the times when his travels had taken him to New York.

Turning back to Hank with a bright smile, she said, "I just hoped I might have inherited some of his natural ability when it came to riding."

"Hey, you can't expect to be an expert horsewoman after one ride."

An expert, no. But she'd hoped for some kind of natural ability. Something that would prove she was not just her mother's daughter, but her father's as well.

"And in my experience, natural ability only takes you so far. The rest is all hard work and determination."

"And let me guess," she said, trying to ignore the hurt. "As a city girl, you don't think I'm capable of either."

He let out a laugh. "Sweetheart, I think you've got more grit and determination than any woman I've ever met!"

The unexpected compliment took Gemma completely by surprise. Knowing Hank saw something in her—something worth admiring, something worth keeping—was almost as much of a gift as finding that old box of photos and postcards had been.

Reaching up on tiptoes, Gemma placed her hands on Hank's broad shoulders. She aimed a kiss at his cheek, but at the last second, he moved. Their lips met and clung. The intimate contact should have taken her by surprise, but how could it when she'd been wondering for days what it would be like to be kissed by a cowboy? Not just any cowboy, but *this* cowboy.

And could he kiss!

Like the man himself, Hank's kiss was an intoxicating mix of tenderness and strength. His lips were soft against hers, but there was no hesitation in his touch, no uncertainty in his claim. He kissed like a man who knew what he wanted, and oh, how Gemma wanted!

So much so that it was her own desire, her own unexpected need, that had her breaking the kiss. Breathless, Gemma gazed up at him. "Okay, I didn't mean to do that."

Despite the desire darkening his gaze and his own unsteady breathing, Hank's mouth kicked up in a grin. "You accidentally kissed me?"

"I meant to kiss you on the cheek."

"You missed."

"You moved." The echo of their conversation on the nature walk had Gemma fighting a smile. Beneath the teasing, though, desire simmered just below the surface. No longer wondering *what if* but knowing and now wondering *what next*. A kiss that amazing, that magical, certainly couldn't be a onetime thing. Not when every brush of Hank's lips against hers and every seductive stroke of his tongue had her straining for more.

As if reading her mind, Hank grinned, his smile sexy enough to make Gemma long to grab him again. Only, next time she'd make sure there would be no mistaking her intentions!

After a half hour or so of walking through the calf-high grasses, spotting a cluster of wildflowers here and there, Hank led the way back to the tied horses. He'd told her he wanted to give the animals a chance to rest, but Gemma had the feeling he was thinking more about giving her backside a break.

The afternoon was so peaceful, with only the sound of the rushing waterfall and the chirp of a bird or a buzzing insect. They walked side by side, close enough that their arms occasionally brushed, the innocent touches enough to strike sparks of awareness along Gemma's skin. When she stumbled on a rock hidden in the grass, he caught her hand to help her regain her balance and then didn't let go.

"We should probably head back," he said finally, and Gemma hoped she wasn't imagining the reluctance in his voice. "I want to be at the hotel when Janie's finished with her kids' outing."

Gemma stopped short, giving his hand a sudden tug.

"Oh, that reminds me! I can't believe I almost forgot to tell you."

"Tell me what?"

"About Janie's master plan."

His hand slid from hers as he asked, "Janie has a master plan?"

"Yep, and talk about grit and determination..."

By the time Gemma finished telling Hank about his daughter's plan to find him a wife, he looked twice as shocked as she'd been and ten times more embarrassed. He stripped off his hat and slapped it against his thigh. "I can't believe she actually thought of doing something like that! I remember when Zach ran those ads. From what I heard, the newspaper office was buried with letters from women all looking to become Mrs. Dalton." He swore again beneath his breath. "Hell, I don't know what would be worse. Getting all those letters—or not getting any."

A man like Hank advertising for a wife? The mail room would be snowed under with responses from eager-and-willing women!

"And despite the stunt he pulled with the wedding punch, Homer really is harmless...but still. I guess I should be glad she wasn't old enough to come up with her master plan during the Gal Rush."

"The what?" Gemma asked with a startled laugh.

"After the flood several years ago, we had a minor population boom with workers and volunteers who came to help with repairs. Word got out that Rust Creek Falls had its fair share of single cowboys and that led to a rush of women coming to town."

"Really?" Lissa Roarke's blog posts about the way the whole town pulled together after the disaster had captured Gemma's imagination. But she hadn't read anything about a Gal Rush.

"Yep, enough to form some kind of Newcomers Club. Of course just about all of them have gotten married by now."

"So the Newcomers Club turned into the Newlywed Club?"

Hank managed a chuckle as he settled his hat back in place. "Not sure if they formed an official club, but Rust Creek Falls had its share of weddings then, and even recently."

"And none of those single, new-to-town women snapped you up?" Gemma blurted out, remembering too late that his ex-wife was one of those recent newlyweds.

Hank lowered his head, the brim of his cowboy hat hiding his face, but Gemma still sensed she'd embarrassed him. "I'm old enough to be their father."

"Oh, come on! I don't believe that!"

"Okay, maybe I just *feel* that old. I haven't been out on a date in—he—heck—" he cleared his throat "—I don't know how long."

Gemma fought a grin at the way he'd censored himself. All part of the gentlemanly package that made Hank Harlow such a catch, even if he didn't seem to know it.

"I probably shouldn't be admitting that, should I? I'm no good at this." He pinned her with a look that had Gemma's heart skipping a beat.

"You're better than you know."

He snorted at that. "I'm as rusty as an old nail."

Gemma choked a little. If that kiss was any indication of Hank's skill when he was rusty, then she could only imagine—in great and glorious detail—what he'd be capable of with some polish and practice.

Talk about natural ability!

And maybe Hank didn't have all the smooth come-ons

and easy charm of a ladies' man, but as far as Gemma was concerned, he was all the more attractive for it.

"Not that horses and cattle care much one way or the other, but Janie... When her—when Dan came back to town and got together with her mother, it took a while for Janie to get used to the sudden change in, well, all of our lives."

"Even though you were divorced, Janie was probably worried about another man trying to take your place."

Hank ducked his head until the shadowed brim of his hat hid his face. "She wasn't the only one."

"You're her father. Nothing's going to change that."

Though she'd intended to ease the frown gathering across his forehead, at her words, tension drew his brows closer together. "Yeah, right."

"Hank..."

He walked over to the horses and gathered their reins. "Anyway, we've worked things out, and Janie has accepted Dan. She can see how happy he makes her mother. Now she has it in her head that I need to find someone, too."

"It's sweet that she worries about you."

"She's a kid. I don't want her worrying about anything. But all her talk about me finding someone, going out, has made me realize just how long it's been."

He ran a palm along Hondo's neck. His hands were wide and scarred. So strong and capable, he was not a man who would accept failure—especially not in something as important and fundamental as his marriage. She wasn't surprised he hadn't gotten over the loss easily.

Though she had no right to the emotion, Gemma couldn't help feeling jealous of a woman who once had such a strong hold on Hank's heart. She had no idea what it would be like to have a man so committed to her. Chad certainly hadn't been.

"We're quite a pair, aren't we? It's been too long since your divorce and not nearly long enough since my broken engagement."

Hank's blue eyes narrowed. "So you and your ex—"

Gemma shook her hair back with a toss of her head. "Over. Done. Believe me. But I'm nowhere near ready to get back into any kind of a serious relationship. I'm just here for a Wild West vacation and to have some fun. So, what do you think, cowboy? Is one week enough time to knock some of that rust off?"

Chapter Six

"Hey, kiddo!" Hank grinned as Janie streaked across the hotel lobby, a huge smile on her face. "How was camp today?"

"It was so much fun! We went on another hike, then had lunch before we went fishing down by the creek. Dad, you wouldn't believe it." Giving a dramatic eye roll, she said, "Half the kids didn't even know how to bait their own hook. Not even the boys!"

Having grown up on a ranch, Janie could probably have shown the Maverick Manor guides a thing or two. Still, Hank pointed out, "Not everyone is lucky enough to live around here. This is new to a lot of kids."

Janie shrugged a slender shoulder. "Yeah, I know." Some of her enthusiasm dimmed a little as she chewed on her lower lip, a sure sign she was holding something back. "There was this one kid…"

"Oh, yeah?" Hank asked casually.

"A boy."

"Oh, yeah?" Not so casually this time. "What boy?"

"His name's Bennett, and he's from Chicago. I told him I could show him how to bait his hook, but he got mad and told me he could do it himself. But, Dad—" Janie looked up at him, her blue eyes wide and a little confused "—he really couldn't."

"Well, Janie…" *That's because boys are idiots and you should stay far, far away from them until you're at least thirty. Maybe thirty-five.*

Despite his instant switch into overprotective-dad mode, Hank managed to swallow the warning. "It can be hard for guys to admit they don't know how to do something."

At least most guys. Unlike him. He'd managed to blurt out all of his own failings that afternoon with Gemma. He held back a groan as his own words rebounded back with all the force of a sonic boomerang.

I'm no good at this.

Geez, he must have sounded as awkward and imma-ture as that worm-fearing boy in Janie's kids' camp. How was that for smooth? Telling the first woman to catch his eye in ages how out of practice he was. His own daughter thought he needed the help of Homer Gilmore's spiked wedding punch!

No wonder Gemma had rushed off as soon as they got back to the hotel. Oh, sure, she'd said she'd had a good time and then commented that she needed to take a shower. "I smell like horse," she'd told him with a laugh.

Hank thought she smelled like wildflowers and sun-shine, but even he knew enough not to say *that* out loud. But it was Gemma's words that had stuck in his mind, corralling his thoughts like one of his best cattle dogs.

Is one week enough time to knock some of that rust off?

His blood had headed due south when she issued that challenge. With his tongue stuck to the roof of his suddenly dry mouth, he hadn't found the words to respond. Instead her offer had hung in the warm summer air too long, and the moment had drifted away like campfire smoke. And even though she'd changed the subject and they'd kept up a casual conversation on the ride back, her question lingered—a slow-burning ember that would only take a spark to ignite.

If he was willing to take the risk of getting burned.

Janie huffed out a sigh. "Boys can be so dumb sometimes."

Holding back a sigh of his own, Hank thought, *You've sure got that right, Janie.*

"But what about you and Gemma? Did you have fun? What horse did she ride? Did she have fun? What are you doing for your next date?"

"Okay, it wasn't a date."

And, hell, he was probably making far too big of a deal out of the whole thing. Because it had been so long for him, everything about the idea of dating—everything about Gemma—seemed so new and fresh and appealing. As different as the two of them were, though, after another date or two some of that newness and shine would wear thin.

They'd likely discover they had nothing in common, and before long Gemma would head back to her far more exciting life in New York. Her time in Rust Creek Falls— and whatever time she spent with him— would be like some cheesy souvenir from the hotel gift shop. A memory to bring out and smile over for a moment or two before sticking it in a closet or back on a shelf to gather dust.

But until then…what would be the harm in showing Gemma around town, playing a part in that Wild West experience she was looking for and, yes, knocking some of that rust off?

"Daaaad." Janie's exasperated sigh dragged on long enough for Hank to make up his mind.

"I'll give Gemma a call and see if she wants to have dinner with us tonight. What do you think about that, kiddo?"

Janie's eyes widened as something over his shoulder caught her eye. "I think she already has plans."

Hank turned and felt his jaw drop, right along with every other guy's around, as Gemma glided through the lobby. She'd traded in the jeans and Western shirt she'd bought at Crawford's General Store for an outfit that could only come from New York.

Shimmering silver knit sparkled beneath the lobby's antler chandelier, the wide neckline exposing her collar-bones and shoulders, while the thin material hugged her breasts and skimmed her thighs. Hank knew little about women's fashion, but he wasn't even sure if the thing was supposed to be a long sweater or an incredibly short dress. Gemma did have leggings on beneath, but the black fabric only accentuated the long legs that ended in a pair of shiny black boots that were clearly not intended for horseback riding. She'd piled her dark hair high onto her head, adding an extra level of sophistication.

A wet-behind-the-ears bellhop barely missed crashing a loaded luggage cart into the river-stone hearth of the immense fireplace as Gemma walked by, but Hank couldn't blame the kid. His boots felt rooted to the floor, which was probably the only thing that kept him from tripping over his own two feet.

It was Gemma's stride that faltered, though, as she first caught sight of them. But she smiled brightly as she walked over. "Hey, Janie, how was the nature walk?"

"It was fun," his daughter answered with far less enthusiasm than she'd shown when he asked the same question a few minutes earlier.

Gemma's smile wavered a bit at the lukewarm response. "Oh, well, you'll have to tell me all about it."

Janie's eyes lit at that. "Tonight?" she asked hopefully.

"Oh, I'm sorry, sweetie. I can't tonight." Glancing his way, Gemma fingered one of the long silver tassel earrings that hung nearly to her naked shoulders. "Natalie called. She's heading over to the Ace in the Hole and asked me to join her."

He should have known telling Natalie Crawford she couldn't do something would be tantamount to waving a starting flag in front of her face. But that she would drag Gemma along with her...

"Gemma." His voice sounded rough to his own ears. "I meant what I said earlier. It really isn't a good idea to go there by yourself."

"Well, I didn't come all the way to Montana to sit in my suite alone, and I'm getting pretty good at going places by myself." Giving him a pointed look, she added, "Even if I would rather have someone with me."

"So, seriously, you're here on your honeymoon alone?"

A few days ago, Gemma would have cringed to be put so thoroughly on the spot. But the sheer respect written in Natalie Crawford's expression, coupled with a few Montana Mules—the Ace in the Hole's twist on the classic drink—had her grinning instead. Holding up her copper mug in a toast, she raised her voice over the loud country twang from the jukebox. "Yep, honeymoon for one, please!"

Natalie clinked her glass against Gemma's before she leaned back on her bar stool. "Oh, that is gutsy! I knew I liked you even before you took on Hank Harlow for trying to pay for your clothes."

"His heart was in the right place," Gemma murmured into her mug.

Natalie snorted before taking a swallow of margarita. "With most guys, I'd tell you heart has nothing to do with it, but with Hank… Yeah, you're probably right. He's one of the good guys."

Too good to accept her impulsive proposition. Gemma cringed a little when she thought of her ridiculous offer. The whole thing sounded like some kind of horribly cheesy come-on.

"So, what's his story anyway?" The words escaped Gemma's mouth—courtesy of the vodka in the Montana Mule—but she didn't wish them back. Eyeing the copper mug, she thought, *In for a penny…* "I've already met Janie, and I know he's divorced, but—"

"But what?" Natalie asked.

"But I don't get it," Gemma confessed. "I mean, unless I'm missing some pretty big flaws, he seems like a really great guy."

"He is."

"And he told me how there was some kind of Gal Rush with all these single women who came to town after the flood, and yet he's still single." Gemma shook her head. "It doesn't make sense."

"Nope, sure doesn't. Just like it doesn't make any sense for a gorgeous, smart, sophisticated woman from New York to be in little ole Rust Creek Falls. On her honeymoon. By herself."

Natalie lifted her beer and an eyebrow in question. When Gemma stayed silent, the blonde let out a sigh before turning the conversation back to Hank—much to Gemma's relief and abject curiosity.

"How did the two of you even meet?" Natalie asked.

"He's staying at Maverick Manor."

Gemma supposed she should have waited until her new friend finished taking a drink before making that statement. Natalie nearly choked on her margarita, coughing so hard, she had to wipe tears from her eyes with a small cocktail napkin. "Seriously?" she asked as she waved off Gemma's offer of some water.

"He and Janie are staying there this week. Why? Is it really that hard to believe?" she asked, feeling suddenly defensive—protective, even—on Hank's behalf.

"The guy hardly leaves the ranch other than to come into town when he has Janie for weekend visitation, so for him to stay away for an entire week… Yeah, it's stepping pretty far outside of his box. But if it was Janie's idea… Well, everyone knows he'll do just about anything for that girl."

Even take Gemma horseback riding. He wouldn't have asked her out if not for Janie's persistence. But she could hardly get upset when it was really all so sweet that he was willing, as Natalie put it, to go so far outside of his box to please Janie. And also so sad…to think of Hank isolating himself on his ranch, working so hard, with only his visits with his daughter to brighten his week.

Gemma already knew how far he would go to make Janie happy, but what was it, she wondered, that would make Hank happy?

She lifted her glass and took another drink. The ginger-and-lime concoction fizzed against her lips, a tingle that couldn't begin to compare with Hank's kiss, and she wondered if a week would be enough time to find out.

One beer, Hank told himself as he stepped through the Ace in the Hole's swinging doors. Music, laughter and the hoppy scent of beer assailed his senses as he took a moment to let his eyes adjust to the bar's dim lighting.

Try as he might, he hadn't been able to get the image of Gemma by herself at the Ace out of his head. Oh, sure, he knew Natalie would be there as well, but that did little to ease the churning in his gut. And Janie had seemed to know it.

"You should go, Dad," his suddenly mind-reading daughter had piped up after they'd shared room service, her expression far too serious and knowing for her age.

I want to.

"You know you want to."

Get out of my head, kid! Sucking in a deep breath, Hank told her, "What I want is to be here with you."

His daughter had rolled her eyes. "It's movie night tonight in one of the ballrooms for all the kids and families."

"See, that'll be fun."

Another eye roll. "They're playing *Shrek*."

A movie they had both seen dozens of times. "Perfect. That's a great movie." Only, at the moment the cartoon mirrored his life a little too closely for comfort.

The Bar H wasn't exactly a swamp, but Hank had hidden out there for years under the disguise of working hard and building up the ranch. There was no outside threat to his home, but Gemma with her smile, her humor and her willingness to try posed an even greater threat to his solitary lifestyle.

You should go. You know you want to.

"Gemma doesn't need saving." He didn't realize he'd spoken aloud until Janie frowned at him.

"Huh?"

"Nothing. I just meant that Gemma's fine on her own and out having fun with her new friend."

"You're her new friend, too."

Was he? Did that kiss make them more than friends?

"I don't want to leave you by yourself. This is your vacation, Janie."

"Mr. Crawford has already asked me and some of the bigger kids to watch the little kids. I don't need a baby-sitter." Her chin lifted to a proud angle. "I *am* the baby-sitter."

And with that, Hank's last excuse had flown right out the manor's windows.

So he'd have one beer while he checked to make sure Gemma was okay, and then he would call it a night and head back to the hotel. Hopefully with Gemma in tow. He'd feel better knowing she was back at Maverick Manor. Which even he had to admit made no sense. Gemma was not only a grown woman, but a woman who lived on her own in New York City. She could certainly handle anything a small town like Rust Creek Falls might dish out and then some.

Face it, his subconscious taunted, *you aren't worried that Gemma won't be able to handle the local cowboys. You're jealous she* will.

Ignoring the annoying voice, Hank made his way into the Ace, his boots crunching on discarded peanut shells as he sidestepped a couple of rowdy cowboys arguing over who would buy the next round.

Is one week enough time to knock some of that rust off?

Hank didn't know about the rust, but in a matter of days Gemma had certainly managed to shake him up. He couldn't get the green-eyed beauty out of his mind. And it was more than looks. In recent years Rust Creek Falls had had its share of attractive, single women hit town. But none of them had captured his attention the way Gemma had with her fearlessness and determination in going on a honeymoon by herself, in grabbing the reins on her first horseback ride, in...

Learning to line dance.

Hank stopped short amid the locals clustered around the high-top tables and waitresses weaving their way through the crowed bar, and he stared at the parquet dance floor.

Surrounded by a dozen or so other dancers, Gemma sparkled amid the denim- and plaid-wearing crowd. But it wasn't the silver sweater or the metallic gleam of the earrings dangling from her ears, even though both caught the meager gleam of light from the neon beer signs and multiple televisions hanging around the bar. No, Gemma's glow came from within, and Hank couldn't look away. She was smiling as she dipped a bare shoulder forward and then rocked back in time with the other dancers. But then she tipped her head back and laughed as she turned wrong, bumping into the dancer beside her rather than shimmying the other way.

Not that the guy seemed to mind. Hank's jaw clenched as a familiar cowboy turned Gemma's misstep into an impromptu spin and dip right in the middle of the rest of the choreographed line dancers. Gemma laughed again as her partner drew her into his arms, smiling up at the handsome cowboy.

Suddenly, staying for even a single beer seemed like one too many, but before Hank could back out the door, a female voice called his name. Natalie broke away from a group gathered near the bar and skirted around the crowded high-top tables to reach his side. He didn't have a chance to greet her before she grabbed him by the forearm and started dragging him toward the bar.

"It's about time you got here," she shouted above the music blaring from the jukebox.

"What?"

"I said—"

"No, I heard what you said. I just— I never told Gemma I was coming here tonight."

Natalie rolled her eyes at that. "You're a smart man, Hank, and letting a woman you're interested in come to the Ace by herself would be nothing but dumb."

Hank opened his mouth to argue, but that too would have been nothing but dumb and not something Natalie would have believed for a second. Fortunately the bartender picked that very moment to ask what he wanted, so the only words to come out were his request for a beer.

One beer...

He was halfway through the bottle by the time Gemma made her way off the dance floor—with the grinning cowboy hot on her fancy heels. A few tendrils of dark hair had escaped her intricate hairstyle to frame her face, and she was slightly breathless from dancing. Her eyes lit as she caught sight of Hank, giving both his ego and the desire building inside of him a sudden boost.

"Hank, I didn't think you were coming!"

Natalie caught his eye over Gemma's bare shoulder, and even in the bar's dim lighting he could see her mouth the word *dumb.*

Turning his attention back to Gemma, Hank said, "Well, I've already heard you sing. I figured I shouldn't miss out on watching you dance."

"What's that about singing?" the dark-haired cowboy with her echoed.

"It's nothing." Gemma shook off his question with a smile. "Hank's just teasing me."

But that smile told Hank it was far more than nothing.

It was a private joke between the two of them, and one that Gemma didn't want to share with her line-dancing friend.

To his credit, the cowboy took it all in stride. Holding out his hand, he said, "Garrett Dalton."

Ah, so that was why the guy looked familiar. He was one of the Dalton cousins who'd moved to Rust Creek Falls after their ranch outside of Hardin had been lost in a tragic fire. They'd come to Rust Creek Falls to rebuild and had bought a patch of land that had been a former train depot. Hank had met Garrett's father and a few of his ranching brothers, but from what he'd heard about Garrett, the guy was usually elbow-deep in an engine, working beneath the hood of whatever car, truck or tractor that needed repair. He had a reputation for liking fast cars...and fast women.

"Hank Harlow," he greeted the other man, refusing to give in to the urge to turn the handshake into some kind of macho show of strength.

Garrett's eyebrow lifted. "I've heard good things about the Bar H."

"Thanks," Hank said as he waited for the familiar feeling to come over him. The antsy, impatient need to return to the ranch, the one that hit him anytime he was away for too long. Ranching was a twenty-four-hour-a-day, three-hundred-and-sixty-five-day-a-year commitment, a desire that ran in his blood, bone-deep in his DNA.

But for the first time in longer than he could remember, the Bar H wasn't at the forefront of his mind.

The idea that anything—or anyone—could distract him from what was his lifeblood sent a tremor of unease beneath his feet—like the distant rumble of an oncoming stampede. Taking another swallow of beer, Hank shook off the feeling. The newness of his time away from the

"4 for 4" MINI-SURVEY

We are prepared to **REWARD** you with 2 FREE books and 2 FREE gifts for completing our MINI SURVEY!

FREE
Value Over
$20!

You'll get...

TWO FREE BOOKS & TWO FREE GIFTS

just for participating in our Mini Survey!

Dear Reader,

IT'S A FACT: if you answer 4 quick questions, we'll send you **4 FREE REWARDS!**

I'm not kidding you. As a leading publisher of women's fiction, we value your opinions… and your time. That's why we are prepared to **reward** you handsomely for completing our mini-survey. In fact, we have 4 Free Rewards for you, including 2 free books and 2 free gifts.

As you may have guessed, that's why our mini-survey is called **"4 for 4"**. Answer 4 questions and get 4 Free Rewards. It's that simple!

Thank you for participating in our survey,

Pam Powers

To get your 4 FREE REWARDS:
Complete the survey below and return the insert today to receive 2 FREE BOOKS and 2 FREE GIFTS guaranteed!

"4 for 4" MINI-SURVEY

1 Is reading one of your favorite hobbies?
☐ YES ☐ NO

2 Do you prefer to read instead of watch TV?
☐ YES ☐ NO

3 Do you read newspapers and magazines?
☐ YES ☐ NO

4 Do you enjoy trying new book series with FREE BOOKS?
☐ YES ☐ NO

YES! I have completed the above Mini-Survey. Please send me my 4 FREE REWARDS (worth over $20 retail). I understand that I am under no obligation to buy anything, as explained on the back of this card.

235/335 HDL GNU7

FIRST NAME	LAST NAME

ADDRESS

APT.#	CITY

STATE/PROV.	ZIP/POSTAL CODE

READER SERVICE—Here's how it works:

ranch was still a novelty. In another day or two, he'd be itching to be back on the Bar H and back in the saddle.

Reassured that he had nothing to worry about, Hank said, "Congratulations on finding your new place."

"My aunt and uncle were nice enough to let us all crash at their ranch, but that was a lot of Daltons under one roof. Enough about me, though," he said with a nod to the bartender, who handed him a beer. Pointing the bottle in Gemma's direction, he said, "I want to know what a beautiful woman like you is doing in Rust Creek Falls and how it is that we haven't met before now."

Seeming more amused than anything by the cowboy's charm, Gemma said, "I'm here on vacation and staying at Maverick Manor for the next week."

"Is that right?" Garrett's eyes seemed to light up at that, and Natalie gave a quick laugh.

"Watch out for this one," she warned Gemma. "One week is longer than Garrett's last three relationships combined. Isn't that right, Dalton?"

Instead of taking offense, the dark-haired cowboy grinned as if Natalie showered him with praise. "Hey, if you do it right, you can pack a whole lotta living into a little bit of time."

The bold statement sounded like something Gemma would agree with, but when Hank glanced over, she wasn't looking at the newcomer cowboy. Instead her gaze snagged Hank's as she lifted the copper mug.

"I certainly hope so," she agreed before catching a waitress's eye and waving her over. "Hank will have another drink."

Lifting his bottle, he was surprised to realize it was almost empty. "I only came for one beer," he protested.

Gemma shot him a look that heated his blood. "This one's on me," she told the waitress, who headed for the bar to place the order. Leaning closer to be heard over a new song, she murmured, "I've been told I need to buy a guy a drink first."

"First?" He was almost—hell, make that totally—afraid of what came next.

As if reading his mind, she grinned. "Don't worry, cowboy. I promise to go easy on your...toes. Come on. It'll be fun."

Tilting her head toward the dance floor, she held out her hand. The moment her slender fingers wrapped around his palm, Hank knew he would have followed her anywhere.

"Let me guess," Hank said as Gemma led the way toward the couples moving in time to the music. "Dancing the two-step is part of the Wild West vacation you planned."

"I've always wanted to learn."

"So why haven't you before now?"

"Because before now I've never had you to teach me."

Gemma had no doubt Garrett Dalton could show her a few moves, on the dance floor and off, but there was no other man Gemma wanted guiding her across the rough wooden floors. His hand was hot against her hip, or maybe that was only the blood in her own veins as he pulled her into his arms.

"So, what else is on this list of yours?"

"Oh, you know," Gemma said, realizing how her list had evolved. What she did didn't matter as much as whom she did it with.

Learn to two-step...with Hank. Go for a hayride...with Hank. Sleep beneath the stars...with Hank.

Chad had broken her trust, making her question her own judgment, and he'd done a number on her self-confidence as well. Making her wonder what it was about her that wasn't enough.

But as she met Hank's gaze—the startling blue much more vivid in the garish glow of the neon beer signs—Gemma knew she wasn't imagining the desire reflected there. Nor could she shake the feeling that when Hank looked at her, he saw her. Not just the perfect hair and makeup, not just the designer clothes and flashy jewelry. Instead he saw past all that to the real Gemma inside…and he still liked what he saw.

Which wasn't to say that meeting his gaze didn't leave her feeling more than a little vulnerable. Needing to turn the tables a bit as he guided her through the steps of the dance, she teased, "You've been holding out on me, cowboy. You're good at this."

He ducked his head ever so slightly, and despite the dim lighting, Gemma sensed she'd embarrassed him. The reason dawned with a bittersweet glow and brought a smile to her lips. "You've been practicing with Janie."

Hank cleared his throat even as he maneuvered out of the way of a swing-dancing couple. "Yeah, well, she, um, likes to dance. Always has…ever since she was a little girl."

Gemma could picture it—Janie as a toddler, her tiny fingers wrapped around Hank's broad thumbs, her bare feet on the tops of his boots as father and daughter waltzed together.

"You're a nice guy, Hank Harlow," she whispered around the sudden lump in her throat. "Anybody ever tell you that?"

No wonder he hadn't taken her up on her offer for what could only be a short-term fling.

If that even was what she was offering.

Despite her big-city experience, Gemma had never been one to fall in love—or into bed—easily. An all-girl prep school had limited her teenage opportunities, and then Gemma had thrown herself into her college classes. She'd dated casually after graduation, but her dedication to her career had made sustaining a relationship difficult. And then she met Chad, who'd seemed so perfect, she should have realized he was too good to be true. Unlike Hank, who was as genuine as they came. She'd come to Montana to play cowgirl, but Hank was the real deal.

"People tell me that all the time." A wry smile lifted one corner of his mouth in a sexy smile as he turned her in an intricate circle.

Gemma wasn't surprised. What did surprise her was how quick she was to believe it was true. Chad's betrayal should have scarred her—maybe not forever, but certainly longer than a few weeks. And yet Gemma believed that Hank was someone she could trust, someone she could believe in, someone she could...

Fall in love with?

The startling thought had barely crossed her mind when a female voice called out Hank's name. He froze at the sound, and Gemma looked over to find a wide-eyed, petite blonde staring at the two of them from the edge of the parquet dance floor.

"Oh, um..." Hank cleared his throat. "Hey, Anne. What are you doing here?"

The woman nodded toward a table in the corner that was surrounded by a group of women whispering back and forth and glancing toward the dance floor. "An impromptu girls' night out. Jamie decided Fallon needed a break, so here we are."

"Here we are," Hank echoed.

The moment was growing more awkward by the second, and many women might have been tempted to retreat, but Gemma figured most women hadn't walked in on their fiancé in bed with their best friend. She and embarrassing situations were well acquainted. Holding out a hand, she said, "Hi, I'm Gemma Chapman."

"Anne Stockton. It's nice to meet you." Despite the slightly puzzled frown pulling her pale brows together, Anne's words seemed genuine. "How do you and Hank know each other?"

"We're both staying at Maverick Manor."

"Oh, of course." Anne smiled as if that explained everything, even though Gemma wasn't so sure it did. At least not from where she was standing.

"They're having a movie night for the kids at the hotel," Hank added. "Nate Crawford asked Janie if she would help keep an eye on some of the younger kids."

Anne nodded. "She'll love that. Well, Gemma, it was nice to meet you. Have a good time tonight, you two."

The blonde headed back to her table, but even though Hank guided Gemma through the steps of the dance, the easy rhythm and seductive sway of their bodies was missing now. Suddenly it was as though they had four left feet, and Gemma couldn't keep quiet any longer. "I broke off my engagement because my fiancé was sleeping with my best friend."

Gemma didn't know whose left foot Hank stumbled over, but he barely caught himself before they both hit the floor. Swearing beneath his breath, he muttered, "Geez, Gemma, that's— I'm so sorry that happened to you."

The sincerity in Hank's gaze reminded Gemma of why she'd felt he was a man she could believe in, a man she could trust. "I really have no interest in being a third wheel, so if you and Anne have something going on—"

"Gem…" Blue flame sparked in his eyes as he shook his head. "I am not your ex-fiancé. And I am not engaged, and I am not married."

"But Anne…"

Hank sighed. "Anne is Janie's mother," he admitted, "and my ex-wife."

His ex-wife.

Hank's words were still ringing in Gemma's ears as the music changed to a faster beat, and they both agreed to head back to their table. Natalie and Garrett had taken to the dance floor, leaving them the spot to themselves. Although Gemma didn't exactly feel like it was just the two of them. Though she tried not to, she shot a glance over to Anne's table. Not only Anne, but all of her friends, seemed equally interested in glancing back at her and Hank.

So much for "What happens at Maverick Manor stays at Maverick Manor."

"What was that?" Hank asked.

Not realizing she'd muttered the words out loud, Gemma shook her head. "I was just thinking… It's so easy to pretend we don't have lives outside of the hotel, but we do. In your case, right outside. I can go back to New York and pick up my life right where I left off, as though nothing has changed…"

Her throat closed over the words. Could she? Could she really go back without feeling like she would be leaving a piece of herself behind?

She waved a hand at the people in the bar. "I'll never see any of these people again," she said, strangely disappointed by that realization, "but you live here."

A slight smile tilted Hank's lips as he set the beer bottle down. "Why, Miss Gemma, are you worried about my reputation?"

"Yes! No. Maybe…"

His deep chuckle had the muscles in her belly clenching. "You know how everyone's always sayin' what a nice guy I am? Well, maybe I wouldn't mind giving 'em something else to say." Gemma figured the gossips would have plenty to talk about as Hank dropped a twenty on the table and tipped his head toward the exit. "You ready to head back?"

If he wasn't worried about the two of them leaving together, then neither was she. Catching Natalie's gaze on the way out, Gemma pointed toward Hank and then the door, letting her new friend know she'd found her own ride back to the manor. The blonde gave an exuberant thumbs-up that had Gemma laughing beneath her breath until she stepped out into the cool night air and found herself alone with Hank.

"The place was busy tonight. I had to park a few blocks away. If you want to wait here, I can go get the truck."

Away from the raucous beat booming from the jukebox, they no longer needed to lean in to hear what the other had to say. And yet Gemma still found herself whisper-close. "There you go again, Mr. Nice Guy."

"Damn." How was it that his deep drawl seemed to stroke every one of her nerve endings? "I really need to work on that, don't I?"

The Ace of Hearts sign in the bar's front window cast a neon glow across his handsome features, and Gemma didn't think he needed to change a thing. From where she stood, Hank Harlow was just about perfect.

The doors swung open as a group of laughing cowboys stumbled outside, and Hank wrapped an arm around her waist, guiding her away from the high-fiving, back-slapping trio and down the quiet street.

"For what it's worth, I can think of plenty of descriptions that go way beyond nice," she said, keeping a teasing note in her voice. "Things like…'That Hank Harlow, he's such a skilled horseman.' Or 'That Hank Harlow, he's such a great dancer.' Or 'That Hank Harlow, he is such an amazing kisser.'"

"Not sure I want the men around here saying that last one, but…"

Gemma laughed even as it struck her that she didn't want the women of Rust Creek Falls saying that either. "So, you and Anne…"

Hank groaned. "Do you really want to talk about my ex-wife?"

Gemma shrugged. "Color me curious."

"That color wouldn't happen to be green, would it?"

"No, of course not!" She was not jealous. At all. But she couldn't help noticing how she and the other woman couldn't have been more different. Anne was blonde and petite, the epitome of a fresh-faced country girl. If Anne was Hank's type…

"We've been divorced for over eight years."

"It seems like you still get along."

"We do. We always have."

"If that's the case, then why did you two get divorced?"

"Because she never loved me."

Gemma stumbled to a stop. The shock of the words, multiplied by Hank's matter-of-fact tone, had her protesting, "Hank, that's—"

Not true. It couldn't be true. How could any woman not fall for a man like Hank?

"I knew it all along. Anne was totally up-front with me. She told me she loved her high school sweetheart and that she always would. I thought I could change her mind, that she would learn to love me. But…love doesn't work that way. Still, I've got Janie, and Anne and I are good friends. I have nothing to complain about."

"You have really got to work harder on that 'not being a good guy' thing."

The glow of the streetlights backlit his rugged silhouette, but Gemma could still see the glint of his blue eyes as he stared down at her. "Right now I'm more interested in working on that 'amazing kisser' thing."

Reaching up, he tilted her face toward his. This time it was no accidental meeting when his lips brushed against hers, and she breathed his name on a sigh. The sound seemed to hover in the charged air between them. A connection drawing them closer until their mouths met again, this time on Hank's hoarse whisper.

"Gemma…"

As he brought his mouth fully down on hers, Gemma decided *amazing* was far too tame a description. She couldn't think of the words for how wild and wonderful he made her feel—and then she couldn't think at all. Her lips parted for the exploration of his tongue, his taste, as he deepened the kiss.

Hank pulled her body tightly against his, closer than when they'd been on the dance floor, but there was still a matched rhythm to their movements—his hands anchoring her hips as her arms wrapped around his shoulders, her head tilting to the side as he deepened the kiss, their hearts beating as one.

He skimmed his lips over her cheeks, forehead and mouth. When he found the skin beneath her jaw, Gemma tilted her head back to offer him full access to her throat. He pressed a kiss there and followed the wide neckline of her sweater where it had slipped down over her shoulder.

His hot breath bathed her skin, and her heart seemed to melt in the heat. It puddled low in her belly without skipping a single pulsating beat. Her nipples tightened even though he hadn't done so much as touch her there. But she wanted him to. Oh, how she wanted him to!

"Hank." She murmured his name in a throaty whisper, but another sound intruded.

Laughter...the beep of a car alarm...the sound of an engine... All reminders that they were standing on a sidewalk not far from—

Gemma blinked as he broke the kiss and the building across the street came into focus.

The sheriff's office.

Getting arrested for breaking some kind of public indecency law was certainly *not* on her vacation to-do list. But as her gaze met Hank's, she thought the risk just might be worth the night in jail. They were both out of breath, but a lack of oxygen did nothing to dampen the fire in his eyes.

"So...how do we do this?" he rasped out.

"This?" He had said it had been a long time, but surely he didn't need her to explain...

He waved a hand between them, and Gemma wasn't sure if he was fanning the flames or trying to put them out. "This one-week thing—or affair—or whatever you call it."

He was asking her? Oh...he was asking her. Gemma swallowed around the sudden lump in her throat. Because of course, as a city girl on a honeymoon for one, she would know all about flings and affairs. And okay, she had started this with her offer to help shake the rust off. So she could either back away now or brazen through like she had ever since walking in on Chad and Melanie.

She could have backed out of Chad's apartment unnoticed. He and Mel had certainly been suitably distracted. Or once she confronted him, she could have believed him when he swore it was a onetime thing and would never happen again. Even once the wedding was called off, she could have taken the time to hide out in her apartment, writing thank-you notes for gifts she had to return and feeling sorry for herself.

Instead she'd slammed that bedroom door open, tossed off her engagement ring and taken that first-class plane ticket to Rust Creek Falls, and she hadn't regretted a minute of it.

So even though the smart thing to do, the thing she *should* do, was to back away, Gemma stood her ground and stayed right where she wanted to be. In Hank's arms. "We hang out. We have fun."

"Mark some more items off that vacation to-do list of yours?"

Her heart stumbled a bit at the sexy suggestion. "And maybe while we're at it, we can figure out what else you're good at." And if his kisses were any indication, Gemma had no doubt that Hank would be as impressive in bed as he was out of it!

"And when—" he gave a soft laugh "—the honeymoon is over?"

Despite the laugh, his blue gaze was serious as he stared down at her in the moonlight. Was he worried that she would fall too far, too fast? Was he thinking of the Gal Rush, Homer Gilmore's wedding punch or the women who had applied through the newspaper to be some cowboy's wife? Gemma couldn't imagine *all* those events had ended happily ever after and without some sort of drama.

"We both know what happens then. You go back to the Bar H and I go back to New York." She lifted a shoulder in a carefree shrug that didn't feel quite as casual as it should have. "After all, what happens in Maverick Manor..."

Chapter Seven

A knock on the door early the next morning took Gemma by surprise. Sitting on the couch, she'd been relishing a cup of steaming hot coffee, along with the equally heated memories of kissing Hank the night before. Her heartbeat quickened as she crossed the small living area. Still wearing a short silk robe over her nightie, she wasn't exactly dressed for company. But if Hank was the unexpected visitor, Gemma was too eager to see him to worry about not looking her best. Which probably said more about her feelings for the quiet rancher than she wanted to admit.

"Just a second," she called out as she took a moment to try to comb through her long hair with her fingers. Figuring that was the best she could do, she gave her head a quick toss and opened the door to find a Harlow standing there…though not the one she'd been imagining.

"Janie!" Though slightly disappointed to find the young girl rather than her father in the hallway, Gemma greeted her with a smile. "How are you this morning?"

Dressed in a pair of jeans and an oversize long-sleeved shirt, Janie practically bounced into the room, where she claimed one of the cushions on the couch. "I wanted to hear if you and my dad had a good time at the Ace in the Hole last night." She hugged a pillow to her chest and looked completely settled in, all eyes and ears.

"I, um…had a really good time," Gemma said and then could have slapped a hand over her mouth when she couldn't stop herself from asking, "What did your dad say?"

Janie slumped back against the padded armrest. "Last night he said it was late and he was tired." Sitting up suddenly, she argued, "But it wasn't that late, and I wasn't tired. But I guess my dad must have been telling the truth because when I woke up this morning, he was still sleeping. And my dad never sleeps in."

"Never?"

"Nope. He's always up before everybody else. He works in the barn before the sun comes up. Then he has breakfast and heads out again. He never even sets his alarm. He says his body knows when there's work to do."

"Well, around here there's no work to do, so he can let himself relax." Gemma hoped that might be the case. She liked the idea of Hank being able to relax and have fun…with her.

Janie wrinkled her nose. "I guess so. I was gonna order room service, but I didn't want to eat by myself, so I thought I'd come see if I could have breakfast with you."

"Do you know what you want to order?" Gemma waved a hand to the leather-bound menu on the coffee table, but Janie's attention locked on something else.

"Oh, my gosh! I love this!" Janie grabbed the bangle bracelet Gemma had left out the night before. She'd started to slide it on her tiny wrist before she stopped and shot a slightly guilty glance in Gemma's direction. "Sorry... My mom and dad always say I should ask before touching somebody else's stuff."

"It's all right. I don't mind if you try it on."

Janie pushed up the sleeve of her shirt and held out her arm to admire the bracelet, even as it slid down nearly to her elbow. "It's a little big."

"A little," Gemma agreed, biting her lip to keep from smiling.

"Still, it's so cool. And that sweater you wore last night, and your earrings! I would die for a pair of earrings like those! Only, guess what?" Another eye roll. "I don't even have pierced ears yet. Everyone still thinks I'm such a baby."

"Your dad told me that Mr. Crawford thought you were grown up enough to ask you to keep an eye on the little kids during the movie last night. How did that go?"

Janie stripped off the bracelet she'd been so enamored with moments earlier and set it back on the coffee table. "It was okay."

"Only okay? Did something happen?"

"No, the little kids were fine."

"The little kids...but maybe not the big kids?"

Janie was silent so long, Gemma didn't think she was going to answer. "There's this boy..." she finally began.

Hank woke with a start, as disconcerted by the sunlight streaming through the curtains as he was by the unfamiliar bed. He recognized the bedroom suite quickly enough, but what time was it?

He swore beneath his breath when he caught sight of the clock on the oak nightstand. Eight o'clock? He hadn't slept this late since he'd needed twenty-two stitches along his ribs after he barely missed getting gored by an angry bull. And that had been well over ten years ago!

Of course it had been longer than that since he'd gone out dancing. Since he'd lain in bed for an entire night, reliving a kiss and aching for more...

Gemma.

Just the thought of seeing her again had his heart racing as he threw back the covers and headed for the bathroom. He wondered what she had planned for today. She could already mark horseback riding and dancing the two-step off her list of vacation "musts." Maybe he could suggest hiking up to Falls Mountain and Owl Rock. Or maybe taking a drive up to Bear Trap Mountain, a nearby ski resort that offered zip-lining.

He grinned around a mouthful of foamy mint toothpaste at the idea. He had the feeling it would appeal to Gemma's sense of adventure. Just the kind of thing she'd want to do on her Wild West vacation, and something Janie would love as well.

After throwing on his usual wardrobe of jeans and a checkered Western shirt, he gave a quick knock on Janie's bedroom door. "Hey, kiddo, time to rise and shine." His voice trailed off as the partially open door swung inward to reveal a rumpled but empty bed.

"Janie?"

Silence greeted him as he stepped back into the suite's small living room and he noticed a piece of paper tucked beneath his phone. Picking up the note, he read that Janie had gone to seek out Gemma. He shouldn't have been surprised. Janie had been relentless the night before, demanding to know if they'd had a good time at the Ace and if they were going out again.

He'd purposefully kept his response vague, not wanting to get her hopes up. He frowned as he set the note aside. Maybe it was his own hopes he was worried about.

Something about Gemma got to him in a way no other woman had. It was crazy to fall so far and so fast for a woman who was leaving town at the end of her vacation. But maybe Garrett Dalton was onto something…

If you do it right, you can pack a whole lotta living into a little bit of time.

And Hank Harlow was all about doing things right.

A few text messages later, Hank met up with Gemma and Janie in the hotel dining room. The two girls grinned at him as he approached, their matched, excited expressions leaving him distinctly uneasy.

No doubt about it. He was setting his alarm tomorrow morning.

"So, what are the two of you up to?" he asked as he braced himself for whatever had put that sparkle in their eyes.

"We're gonna have a spa day! It's a girl thing," she added with a glance at Gemma, who gave a confirming nod.

"Maverick Manor has a pretty impressive array of spa treatments. They offer massages, manicures, pedicures." Gemma paused long enough to regain his wandering attention. "Even Dead Sea mud baths…if you're interested."

Thinking of the mud-bath facial she'd given him on their nature hike, Hank wryly said, "I think I'll pass, thanks."

He wasn't surprised that Gemma would be interested in the froufrou resort amenities, but he cast a questioning look at Janie and asked, "You really want to try that stuff?"

How was it that it seemed like only yesterday that the only mud his little girl had been interested in were the puddles in the backyard following a summer storm? From the time Janie had taken her first few steps in a tiny pair of pink cowboy boots, she'd been his shadow. She loved the ranch and the land and horses as much as he did. Hank didn't know what to make of his daughter's sudden interest in clothes and jewelry.

Janie nodded. "Gemma says it'll be fun."

Catching his eye, Gemma lifted her chin in that same subtle challenge that had gotten him on the dance floor the night before. "Well, she would certainly know."

With as limited as the choices were in the small town, Hank had been to the Ace in the Hole hundreds of times over the years, but he'd never had as much fun as he'd had with Gemma. For all her big-city sophistication, she had a wide-eyed eagerness when it came to experiencing—no, embracing—something new. Her enthusiasm was contagious enough to make Hank feel as though he were two-stepping, or even going horseback riding, for the first time.

Because he was. He was doing all those things for the very first time—with Gemma.

It was a rare thing for Hank to find himself with too much free time on his hands. On the ranch, there was always work to be done—records to maintain, bills to pay, animals to tend to, repairs to be made. So sitting around with nothing to do should have seemed like a luxury. But after hitting the pool for a few laps and then trying out all the fancy machines in the weight room, Hank was back in the hotel room, his butt parked on the couch as he flipped through the countless cable channels filled with nothing but reality shows.

No wonder I don't watch much TV. He wasn't sure

how anyone could stand the stuff. He did come across a Colorado Rockies game, but not even baseball could hold his attention for long.

Though it had only been a few hours since his late breakfast, Hank flicked off the television and grabbed his keys. Within minutes he was back on Broomtail Road, where he pulled up in front of Daisy's Donuts. As he opened the door to the donut shop, the sweet and yeasty scents of freshly baked treats instantly tempted his taste buds.

"Hey, Hank!" Standing behind the counter, Eva Armstrong Stockton's eyes lit as she caught sight of him. The pretty blonde baker grinned. "Look at you spending time with the little people of Rust Creek Falls. From what I've heard, you're taking all your meals at Maverick Manor nowadays."

He groaned at the teasing as he made his way to one of the bar stools. "Still haven't had anything there that can compare to one of your pies."

"Nice try, but flattery won't free you from the local grapevine."

Hank had always known gossip could spread through the small town like wildfire, but he never paid much attention. Probably because until a few years ago, no one would have had reason to talk about him. But then Daniel Stockton had returned to town and word got out that Janie wasn't Hank's biological daughter. After that, people had plenty to say.

Oh, not to his face. But more than a few conversations cut off the moment he walked into the room, and then picked up again behind his back. Not to mention the pity in townsfolk's gazes when they looked at him.

"Are you eating here?" Eva asked as she held up a pot of coffee.

"Sure," he said even though he could practically picture the baker rubbing her hands together in glee. "I'll have the roast beef on rye."

Within minutes Eva had set a plate with a sandwich piled high with medium-rare beef and a steaming side of thick-cut fries in front of him. "So, how's Janie enjoying the hotel? When I saw her last week, she was so excited."

When Dan returned to town, Janie had gained more than a biological father. She'd also discovered a wealth of Stockton aunts and uncles. Eva had wed Dan's older brother, Luke, the previous summer, and now the two of them were running Sunshine Farm—the family ranch owned by the Stockton siblings.

After swallowing one of the salty fries, Hank said, "She's loving it." In between bites of the mouthwatering sandwich, Hank told Eva about the kid-friendly events set up by the hotel.

After hearing about the spa day, Eva sighed with longing. "I think I'm jealous. I'd love to spend a day getting pampered at Maverick Manor."

"Well, I'm not sure Janie knows what she's getting into. She's always been more of a tomboy."

"Plenty of girls, especially around here, start out as tomboys, but their interests start to change once they're teenagers."

Hank supposed Eva could speak from experience, but he knew his daughter. "Not Janie. She'll always be a cowgirl," he argued, uncomfortable with the thought of her changing into someone he couldn't recognize. Someone he wouldn't know how to connect with. "The spa thing is just part of the whole Maverick Manor experience."

"And what about you, Hank?" Eva asked with a spark in her eyes as she refilled his cup. "How are you enjoying all Maverick Manor has to offer?"

"Turndown service is kinda cool. And I never was one for making the bed."

"You are lucky I am not pouring this coffee in your lap." She lifted the pot in warning before she set it aside. "I'm not asking about housekeeping. I'm asking about a certain dark-haired beauty half the town saw you dancing with at the Ace in the Hole last night."

"You mean Gemma?"

"Unless there's some other dark-haired beauty you've been hiding—which would make Garrett Dalton happy. He was in here complaining earlier that you managed to get to Gemma first."

Hank shook his head. "Get to her first," he echoed. "That makes it sound like I called dibs."

"Did you?"

"Gemma's staying at the hotel on her vacation, and I've been showing her some of the sights around Rust Creek Falls. It's really no big deal."

"Right…because you go dancing at the Ace all the time," Eva teased.

"I'm on vacation, too. I'm allowed a night or two on the town."

Eva's gaze gentled as she lost her teasing smile. "You're allowed far more than that. You deserve far more than that."

"Yeah, well, a few nights are all it's going to be. Janie and I are only staying at the hotel until Saturday."

"And Gemma?"

"Gemma's here one more week, but then she'll be heading back to New York."

"And that's it? You just say goodbye?"

"What else can we say? She's here on vacation, Eva."

She dismissed that with a wave of her hand. "When Luke first came back, he was only here for the wed—" Eva bit her bottom lip as she cut herself off.

"He was in town for Dan and Anne's wedding. It's okay to say it. I was there, remember," he said wryly. Not only had he attended his ex's wedding, he'd also given away the bride.

"Of course I remember." Eva gave a small sigh. "It was so sweet, seeing you walk Anne down the aisle."

Yep, that was him all right. Good-guy Hank Harlow.

He certainly hadn't agreed when Anne asked because he was some kind of martyr. Their marriage had been over for some time, and he truly did wish Anne and Dan nothing but happiness. The kind of true happiness that had eluded him for so long, he'd all but stopped looking... until he'd seen Gemma Chapman laid out in a shiny black bikini at Maverick Manor's pool.

The moment he'd taken her hand, he'd felt something spark to life within him. Something that made him realize how he'd simply been going through the motions— alive but not really living. He'd been numb for so long that every moment, every emotion he experienced with Gemma, was like fireworks going off inside of him. All of them big, bright, beautiful...and damn scary.

Because one thing Hank knew about feeling too much was that it made the pain of losing the woman you loved hurt like hell.

But this...thing with Gemma, whatever it was, it wasn't love.

No way. No how. He wasn't going there. Not with a woman fresh out of a painful breakup. Not with a woman who lived halfway across the continent in New York freakin' City. Rubbing the old wound at his side, he reminded himself that he'd learned from his mistakes. He wasn't fool enough to repeat them.

"That was the most fun ever!" Janie announced as she and Gemma left the hotel's spa and headed back toward the lobby. She held out a small hand, admiring her hot-pink manicure. "I can't wait for my dad to see my new look!"

"Me, too." Gemma thought he'd get a kick out of seeing his tomboy daughter's new hairstyle and makeup. But more than that, Gemma simply wanted to see Hank. To spend more time with him. To spend as much time with him as she could before he left Maverick Manor.

"Oh, look! There he is!" Janie didn't wait for Gemma, sprinting across the lobby and weaving her way around a couple weighed down by enormous backpacks, families pushing strollers and porters maneuvering overloaded luggage carts.

Gemma took her time crossing the crowded space, but her smile faded as she caught sight of Hank's expression. She'd expected the look of surprise, but instead of giving way to the proud-papa smile Gemma was used to, his brows pulled together in a frown. Too far away to hear their conversation, she had no trouble reading Janie's body language as her shoulders slumped and her head drooped.

"Excuse me," she murmured to the backpacking pair as she picked up her own pace, but by the time she reached Hank's side, a crying Janie had already pushed past him.

"Janie, wait!" Hank called after his daughter, but she sprinted down the hall without slowing. Cursing beneath his breath, he turned back to Gemma, regret written across his handsome features. "Geez, Gemma..."

She opened her mouth, ready to tell him it would be okay. That he could apologize to Janie and everything would be all right, but he beat her to the punch with a shot that came out of left field.

"What the hell were you thinking?"

"Me?" The accusation in his eyes had her drawing

up to her full height. He'd been so different the past few days that Gemma had almost forgotten how quick he could be to judge, to cast blame. "You knew we were going for a spa day!"

"I thought that meant— Hell, I don't know what I thought. Do I look like a guy who knows what happens during a spa day? Her hair..." He waved a hand at his own overly long locks. "And all that makeup. She looks like..."

His words cut off, and Gemma thought she caught a flash of pain before his expression hardened. "She's still a little girl, Gemma!"

"She's practically a teenager, Hank!" And maybe one Gemma had been hanging out with a little too much, as she was suddenly tempted to copy Janie's eye roll as she echoed the girl's own words. "She's old enough to have an interest in hair and makeup, clothes and boys!"

"I think I know my daughter better than you do. Janie's a tomboy! She likes horses and fishing and spending time on the ranch."

I think I know my daughter...

Gemma had never known her father. Had she known more about him, Gemma might have liked horses and fishing and ranching, too. But she had never had the chance. She'd never had the *choice*. Instead her mother had signed her up for ballet classes, voice lessons and piano recitals.

Gemma was pretty sure her mother thought she knew her, too. Or at least knew the version her mother had molded her into—the wealthy, sophisticated, well-educated daughter of Diane and Gregory Chapman. Diane was all too willing to dismiss any reminders that Gemma wasn't Gregory's biological daughter, packing away whatever memories she might have along with all the pictures of Gemma and her father.

"Yes, she's a bit of a tomboy, but she also likes dresses and makeup and musicals! Maybe she'll grow up to be a cowgirl or maybe she won't. The question is, will you love her enough to let her be whoever, whatever, she wants to be?"

Love her enough?

Who the hell did Gemma think she was, questioning if he loved his daughter enough? Hank hadn't even known what love was until he held Janie in his arms. Gemma didn't have a clue what that felt like, he thought as he followed the path Janie had taken at a slightly slower—if no less furious—pace.

Easy for her with her fancy New York apartment and unencumbered lifestyle to tell him how to relate to Janie! What did she know? What could she possibly know?

But she *did* know.

Gemma might not know what it was like to be a parent, to love a child with her whole heart, to want nothing less than the best for that child. But she knew how it felt to be on the other side. To be the child who hadn't been loved enough.

She hadn't told him much about her past, but what she had told him added up to a lonely childhood. She was a cowboy's daughter, but she didn't know how to ride. Her father had been born in Rust Creek Falls, yet Gemma had never been to Montana. Instead she'd been raised in New York City before being sent off to boarding school. In Connecticut...a hundred miles from home and essentially a million miles from Montana.

Rubbing the back of his neck, he shoved the thought from his mind as he headed back to the suite. He paused in the hallway outside the door as his cell phone rang. The familiar ringtone was one he couldn't ignore, and he didn't even have a chance to greet his ex-wife before Anne demanded, "What is going on, Hank? I just got a call from Janie. She was crying and said she wants to come home."

"Go home?" The words hit like a blow to his gut, and he fought back a curse as he stared at the closed door.

"Janie's been looking forward to this for months, and now she wants to cut her vacation short? What on earth happened, Hank?"

He gave a brief explanation, downplaying Gemma's role as much as he could, although he wasn't even sure why. Because he didn't want Anne to worry that a visitor from New York City was having any kind of influence in Janie's life? Or was it because he didn't want to admit the effect Gemma had already had on his? "I don't know what to do, Annie. Janie's never been this upset with me before," he confessed.

Anne was silent for a long moment, and Hank's hand tightened on the phone as he waited for some words of wisdom. Despite the divorce, he and Anne had always gotten along and had almost always seen eye to eye when it came to Janie. He really needed her help on this one.

Instead he got an earful of laughter. "Welcome to parenthood."

Hank ground his back teeth together as he tried to hold back his anger…and hurt. "I've been a parent since the day that little girl was born, Annie."

Her laughter immediately cut off. "Oh, Hank, I didn't mean it like that. Of course you know what it's like to be a parent, but you and Janie—" She gave a small sigh. "I can't tell you how many times I've envied your relationship with her."

"What? Why? You don't think— I would never try to turn her against you. Or Dan."

"I know that, and I know Janie loves me, but she

adores you. The two of you are so alike and have so much in common that you've always gotten along. But that doesn't mean you aren't going to butt heads once in a while. Especially now that Janie's almost a teenager. And that's all I meant. Parenting isn't always smooth sailing. Remember when Dan first came back and we told Janie he was her father? You were the one she ran to when she decided she couldn't stand to live with me anymore."

Hank hadn't wanted Anne to tell Janie the truth, so his sympathies had definitely been with his daughter and not with Anne or the man who'd shown up after more than a decade to throw all their lives into turmoil. But now… "I feel like crap knowing that she's mad at me."

"So find a way to fix this, and give Janie the vacation she's been dreaming of."

Find a way to fix this…

Easier said than done with Janie locked in the bathroom in their suite. After fifteen minutes of futilely trying to apologize to his daughter through a keyhole, Hank found himself standing on the opposite side of another door. Unlike Janie, Gemma did respond to his knock, but her expression was far from open.

Not knowing what else to do, Hank went with the unvarnished truth. "I screwed up, Gemma. With Janie and with you." Taking it as a good sign that she didn't slam the door right in his face, he asked, "Can I come in?"

As Gemma took a step back, Hank walked inside. Similar to the suite he shared with Janie, the hotel room opened into a small living room. Unlike their room, however, the honeymoon suite offered the romantic touches of a faux-bearskin rug spread out in front of a river-stone fireplace. Beyond a wall of windows, a large balcony overlooked the distant mountains. And through a pair of double doors to the right…

Hank jerked his gaze away but not before the wide canopy bed was burned into his brain. The huge pillows, the fluffy comforter, the silken sheets—all he could imagine was Gemma on the big white bed, her long dark hair spread over the pillowcases, over the sheets. Over him. The mattresses at Maverick Manor were too soft for his comfort, but in that bed, with Gemma in his arms, it would be like making love in the clouds.

"What are you thinking, Hank?"

He started at the question, his guilty gaze snapping toward Gemma, who still stood in front of the door, arms crossed over her chest. "Uh, what?"

"What were you thinking?" she repeated. "Janie was so excited to show you her new look."

Hank was hit by a double dose of guilt. Since stepping foot inside Gemma's suite, he hadn't been thinking of his daughter at all. But now the remembered shock reverberated through him again, knocking the wind from him just as it had when Janie had raced across the lobby. Looking so grown-up, looking just like—

"Hank?" Some of the starch went out of Gemma's shoulders as her arms dropped to her sides.

Shaking off the thought, he told Gemma, "Janie isn't allowed to wear makeup until she's thirteen."

Though she didn't say anything, Gemma's single raised eyebrow spoke volumes. No doubt she felt him as old-fashioned and out of touch, as his daughter had accused him of being. Even to his own ears, the argument sounded stupid because the makeup hadn't been the problem.

Instead of arguing, Gemma stepped closer and said, "I'm sorry, Hank. I didn't know, and I should have talked to you first."

"You didn't know, but Janie did."

"True, but you have to admit, staying at Maverick

Manor is a special occasion. This is a big deal for her, and besides—" Gemma gave a sudden sigh "—there's this boy."

"Wait—this is about some boy?" Hank demanded.

"No," Gemma said with an expression of infinite patience, "this is about *Janie*...with a teeny, tiny dash of mean-girl one-upmanship thrown in."

"Mean-girl...what?"

"Mean girls. You know, the ones who..." Her voice trailed off as she gave him a look of hopelessness she could have copied from his daughter. "You really don't watch much television, do you?" Waving a hand that had her bracelets clinking around her wrist, she said, "Never mind all that. Yesterday, during their kids' outing, Janie offered to help the other kids bait the hooks and show them how to fish."

"Yeah, she told me about that."

"Well, what she may not have told you is that some of the other girls were making fun of her for knowing so much about something that only boys know how to do."

"That's ridiculous." While Hank considered himself every bit the gentleman—and did certainly consider some jobs as belonging to men—there was nothing about casting a line that was too dangerous or demanding for a female to handle. "Girls are perfectly capable of fishing."

"Thank you... I think. But these girls were teasing Janie about being a tomboy. Janie wants to see herself as more of a girlie girl, but she doesn't know where to start. And as much as she loves you, Hank, you are not the person anyone would go to when it comes to being a girlie girl."

"Well, thank you... I think," he said with a smile that faded quickly. He hated the idea of anyone hurting his little girl—even so much as hurting her feelings.

Which, he realized with a quick punch to the gut, was exactly what he had done.

"Yesterday Janie was just a little girl. *My* little girl. And now—"

"Oh, Hank, do you really think a bit of makeup is going to change that? Janie loves you. She will always be your little girl."

"You don't get it, Gemma. You don't know—"

"Know what?"

"Janie isn't mine!"

The words whipped out before Hank could stop them, and Gemma stepped back, flinching at the sharp and sudden recoil. "Janie's...what?"

With the admission sapping the strength out of him, Hank sank onto the couch. "Janie isn't my daughter."

Gemma's green eyes widened, and he expected to see pity shining from their emerald depths. Instead a righteous anger blazed there. "You're saying that Anne—"

Knowing what Gemma was thinking, he shook his head. "She didn't cheat on me, and she never lied. She was pregnant when we met and married. But she told me right up front, so I knew all along."

And he hadn't cared. With all they had in common— their desire to live in a small town, their love of ranch life, their love of animals—Hank had thought Anne would be the perfect wife. And when he learned she was pregnant, that only seemed like even more of a reason for them to wed. "But no one else did. As far as everyone in Rust Creek Falls knew, I was Janie's dad. But then Daniel Stockton came back to town. Back into Anne's life... and into Janie's."

Gemma sucked in a quick breath. "*Her other dad*... When Janie said that, I thought she meant her stepfather."

Hank shook his head. "*I'm* the stepfather, and a former one at that."

"You were—you *are* her father, Hank." Sitting beside him on the couch, she placed a gentle hand on his arm. "Biology isn't enough to erase all those years when you were there for her when her real father was not. You were the one to rock her to sleep and teach her to dance. You were the one to buy her her first pony and show her how to ride."

"I thought I'd worked through all this when Dan first came back two years ago. Hell, I was even the one to walk Anne down the aisle when they got married."

"But now things are changing again," Gemma surmised, surprising him with her insight, though Hank didn't know why. Hadn't she known just what it would take to get him out on the dance floor? And hadn't she sensed what would make Janie, his own daughter, feel more confident and self-assured?

"She calls him 'Dad' now," Hank confessed hollowly, his hands hanging between his thighs. "I mean, there's no reason why she shouldn't. Since he came back, Dan has done everything he said he would. He's been a part of Janie's life, getting to know her, making up for lost time, and he *is* her father. Seeing her today... I always thought she took after Anne. The two of them look so much alike, but when I saw Janie running across the lobby, it hit me. She looks exactly like Dan's sister Bella did when she was a teenager."

He shook his head. "She's a Stockton through and through. There's no denying it." Even though a part of him still wanted to.

"It takes far more than DNA to make a family, Hank. You know that."

"That's what I tell myself. Most days I believe it."

"And those other days?"

"On the bad days, I can't help remembering how it

felt to be married to Anne—knowing she loved another man more, a man who eventually took my place as her husband and as Janie's dad."

Her hand tightened on his arm, the touch no longer gentle but firm with conviction. "I said before that Janie was a lucky girl, and that was before I knew the half of it. My father died before my fourth birthday. I don't have any memories of him, and my stepfather shipped me off to boarding school as soon as he could."

Hank didn't know what to say, even as the missing pieces fell into place. Gemma's father was a cowboy but he'd never had the chance to teach her how to ride. He'd been born in Montana, but he hadn't been around to introduce her to the close-knit community of Rust Creek Falls. And the man who'd had the opportunity—the chance, the *gift*—of taking his place in Gemma's life had sent her away instead. "Gemma…I'm so sorry."

She shook her head. "I'm not telling you this so you'll feel sorry for me. I'm telling you so that you'll realize how blessed Janie is. Yes, she has Anne and Dan, but she has *you*. And she loves you, Hank. Why do you think she's trying so hard to set us up? It's because she worries about you. She knows what a great guy you are. And she knows any woman to catch your eye would be almost as lucky as she is."

Gemma forced herself to meet the summer-sky blue of Hank's gaze as she said the words, unwilling to give away how she wished she could be that lucky. How she wished she could be that woman. Though he might have been a little rusty on the outside, inside Hank Harlow had a heart of gold.

She never would have known, never would have guessed Janie wasn't his daughter. How could she have when he clearly loved her with everything he was? Biology… DNA… Those connections had nothing over heart and soul.

Her own stepfather had never made her feel like anything more than an unwanted by-product of what he called her mother's "youthful indiscretion." A mistake to be sent away—out of sight, out of mind.

As if reading her thoughts, he ran his fingers through her freshly cut hair. He tucked a lock behind her ear before fingering the long chandelier earring she wore. "You look beautiful. I should have told you that."

"You should have told Janie that."

"You're right." His eyes crinkled a bit in a self-deprecating smile, but he sobered quickly. "It's not too late, you know."

"To tell Janie how beautiful she looks?"

Hank shook his head, the intensity in his gaze causing nerves to take flight in her belly. "For you to decide that you like cowboy boots and Stetsons and horseback riding. It's not too late for you to be whoever or whatever you want to be."

He would love her enough to let her be whoever or whatever she wanted to be?

No, that wasn't what he was saying. It was crazy to even think that was what he was saying! Hank was simply being Hank. The good guy who had encouraged her despite her city-girl ignorance.

"What I want…is to be with you." Gemma all but whispered the words. She didn't toss her hair; she didn't flash a smile; she didn't throw down a challenge like she had when she offered to help him shake some rust off. She wasn't trying to hide her hurt, because her honeymoon for one had done more than Gemma might have hoped. Thanks to the handsome rancher seated beside her, it was helping her heal.

You deserve a woman who will love you for exactly who you are.

His blue eyes widened, and for a brief, heart-stopping second, she feared she'd said the words out loud. "I want to be with you, too," he murmured, his deep voice husky as he responded to the words she actually *had* said.

Gemma swallowed against her dry throat as she voiced the word he hadn't spoken. "But..."

He closed his eyes for a moment, and when they opened, a hint of humor had replaced the heat she'd seen shining there. "I've got a ticked-off girl locked in the bathroom of our suite, and I'm really hoping I won't have to call security to break the door down."

In the end, calling security wasn't necessary. The door that had been locked against Hank opened quickly when Gemma asked if she could come in.

"Only you," Janie insisted through the small crack along the jamb. "Not my dad."

Gemma shot Hank a sympathetic but encouraging smile as she slipped into the bathroom. Janie scrubbed at the tears streaking her cheeks as she sat down on the edge of the tub. "I'm not supposed to wear makeup until I turn thirteen," she confessed.

That was something she might have told Gemma sooner, but there was no sense pointing that out now. Reaching over, she plucked a tissue from the holder on the counter before settling onto the tub, beside the girl. "Well, there's something I forgot to tell you, too," she said gently as she passed her the tissue. "There's no crying in makeup. Tears will have that mascara running down your face in no time, and you'll end up looking like a crazy clown."

Just as Gemma hoped, Janie let out a little laugh as

she wiped at her eyes. "I really thought my dad would think I looked pretty."

"Your dad thinks you are beautiful, inside and out, makeup or no makeup. In fact, he told me when he first saw you that he thought you looked just like your aunt Bella."

"Bella's nice and really pretty." Janie's cheeks turned a little pink. "My dad said I looked like her?"

"That's what he told me."

"Everyone always said I looked like my mom but then…"

"Then your other dad came back to town." At Janie's nod, Gemma asked, "Does he have any other brothers and sisters?"

Janie nodded. "There's Luke and Bailey and Jamie and Dana and Liza."

"That's a lot of aunts and uncles."

"I have cousins, too." As Janie told Gemma about her uncle Jamie's triplets, her tears quickly dried. "They're so cute and funny."

"Sounds like you have a really big family."

"Yeah. At first it was weird. I mean, for so long it was just me and my mom and dad…" Janie crumpled the tissue in her hand. "My dad Hank."

"He loves you very much."

"I'm—I'm kinda all he's got, you know."

Gemma's heart ached a bit at the sincerity in the young girl's eyes and at the truth in her words. "I know, so do you think maybe you can forgive him for holding on to you a little too tight?"

At Janie's jerky nod, Gemma went to open the bathroom door to find Hank standing right on the other side. His hair was mussed as he ran his fingers through it for what was clearly not the first time. But it was the look in his eyes—the shadowed reminder of the words he'd spoken earlier—that grabbed hold of Gemma's heart.

Janie's not my daughter.

Gemma could only imagine how devastated Hank must have been when Janie's biological father had returned a few years ago, but by her guess, those shadows stretched far longer than that.

Hadn't she always wondered about her biological father? Even though she'd known he was dead and that he would never be a part of her life, believing for so long that he had never been a part of her life, she had still wondered.

How much worse must it have been for Hank wondering about Janie's father? Knowing the man was alive and well, not just out in the world somewhere but also in his wife's heart?

Oh, Hank...

Just last night they had laid out the terms for their no-strings affair. So why was her heart already urging her to break all the rules?

Chapter Eight

"This is punishment, isn't it?" Hank demanded the following morning. "Even though I said I was sorry, you're both out to torture me. That's just cruel."

Gemma and Janie exchanged smiles at his hangdog expression before they each grabbed an arm and started dragging him from the crowded parking lot. "Come on, Dad. It's just the mall."

"Oh, no!" He gave an exaggerated shudder. "Not the mall!"

Janie giggled and pulled him harder toward the sprawling shopping center. He wasn't one for buying forgiveness, but Gemma's words had stuck with him. If his daughter was growing up, if she was changing from a tomboy to a girl who liked clothes and makeup, then he could man up and be the dad who would take her shopping for those things.

Oh, he had no doubt once Gemma was back in New

York that Janie would likely prefer to make these trips to Kalispell with Anne, but he wanted Janie to know that he would take her. That he would do anything for her.

Even go to the mall.

"Relax, Hank," Gemma said as they stepped through the automatic doors of the largest department store. "It's the middle of the day on a Thursday. It's not like we'll be fighting the Christmas rush."

"Don't remind me," he replied as Janie rushed ahead of them toward the junior section. "I still have nightmares from last December."

"Last-minute shopping?"

"Is there any other kind?"

Gemma shook her head. "Men…will you never learn?"

"I think I might…as long as you're around to teach me." But of course he and Janie were checking out of the hotel on Saturday, and Gemma would only be around for another week. That would be a crash course no matter what subject he was studying. Which, at the moment, was his favorite subject of all. He'd never been much of a student, but he could write essays about the way her dark lashes fanned across her porcelain cheekbones as she lowered her gaze. Compose poetry about the flecks of gold in her emerald eyes. Capture the perfect shape of her lips in any medium possible—sculptor's clay, painter's oils, a photographer's camera. Or best of all, with his own mouth molding, shaping and memorizing her lips with his own.

Seeming all too aware of the quick passage of time, Gemma murmured, "I hope you're a fast learner."

"I think you will find me a highly motivated student."

"Hey, Dad, Gemma, check this out!"

Motivated or not, their lessons would have to wait as they turned their attention to Janie, who was holding up a black-and-white geometric-print shirt, similar to one of Gemma's.

"I love it!" Gemma exclaimed. "Do they have it in my size?"

"No, silly, this one's for me!"

Gemma gave his arm a final squeeze before she headed over to Janie's side. As she tilted her head toward Janie, her long dark hair the perfect contrast to his daughter's short blond locks, Janie's words echoed in his mind.

She's the one for me.

Hank wasn't sure when the two females in his life turned their gazes from the pink- and purple- and floral-draped mannequins and centered on him, but he definitely felt caught in the crosshairs as they steered him toward the menswear section. Janie already had her hands filled with shopping bags after their successful foray into the junior department, and Hank was more than ready to head for the food court or the exit.

"Oh, no!" he protested when he spotted the bizarre headless male mannequins draped in some of the most garish prints he'd ever seen. "No way. Do you have any idea what would happen if I wore a shirt like that on the ranch?" he asked, gesturing toward a hot-pink polo. "I'd lose all the horses' respect, and the cattle would take one look and start a stampede. If I'm going shopping, and that's a big *if*, it'll be at Crawford's."

But Gemma was already shaking her head. "We're not shopping for you at Crawford's."

"That's where I took you."

"Because I needed denim and Western shirts and cowboy boots. You, on the other hand, need something other than denim and Western shirts and cowboy boots."

Janie's giggle punctuated Gemma's statement. "He doesn't wear anything but jeans. Ever."

"Because that's what ranchers wear," he argued as he tossed an arm around Janie's shoulders, "and the last time I checked, the cattle didn't care about my wardrobe."

"Well, try to remember that you aren't dressing for a bunch of cows, and this might not be as painful as you think it will be," Gemma added.

"Oh, it's gonna be painful. I have no doubt about that."

Despite Hank's dragging his heels, they found a saleswoman quickly enough. As Gemma chatted up the woman, he was pretty sure he saw dollar signs flashing in her eyes.

Not that he couldn't afford one of the fanciest suits displayed on the mannequins posed around the store. He could. But where would he even think to wear something like that once Gemma was gone? And unlike Gemma, who seemed so eager to take home mementos of her time in Rust Creek Falls, Hank wasn't going to need those reminders. Once she left, he feared he would see her everywhere he looked—riding beside him on Lightning, picking out Western wear in Crawford's, line dancing at the Ace, kissing him under the stars...

"What do you think about this?" Gemma asked as she gestured toward a slate-blue dress shirt that looked like it would disintegrate the moment he brushed up against a rough piece of wood in the barn.

It wouldn't take long before anything he bought in that store would end up in the back of his closet. Gathering dust—just like he was. But not yet. With Gemma by his side, he felt like he was twenty years old. Younger, even, considering he'd already had the weight of his family's ranch on his shoulders by the time he was in his twenties.

"Think you can shine a rusty old cowboy into a city slicker?"

"I wouldn't even try. City slickers are a dime a dozen. And there isn't a man in all of New York that I'd rather be with than you."

Hank did purchase the shirt, along with two others, a pair of slacks and a tie that Janie had laughingly picked out for him. But as the saleswoman started ringing up his purchases, Gemma placed a hand on his arm. "Are you sure about this, Hank?"

"What? Do you think I should have gone with that other tie instead?"

"No, I mean…it was my idea to go shopping…"

With the sales assistant eyeing the two of them, Hank couldn't help but chuckle. "Didn't we have this argument already? You paid for your clothes. I'll pay for mine."

"But you already went a little overboard with everything you bought for Janie," Gemma argued before meeting the look he gave her with a sigh. "All right, fine. But not the suit," she insisted with a firm look at the saleswoman.

"I thought you liked the suit," Hank murmured as the associate hung the dark slacks and matching jacket on a rack of items to be returned to the floor.

Like the other day at Crawford's when Gemma had modeled the latest in Western wear, Hank had taken his turn in the dressing room. Every time he had stepped out, Gemma had moved in—fixing a collar here, adjusting a sleeve there. The casual touches had been driving him crazy, as had the way Gemma's eyes darkened when she'd taken in the sight of him in the suit.

Even now a husky note entered her voice as she said, "I loved the suit. You looked…" Her words trailed off into a moment of silence filled with all the things they weren't saying. But then, with a small shake of her head, she cleared her throat and added, "But it's too much. You wouldn't have any place in Rust Creek Falls to wear it."

"No, I suppose not," he agreed slowly. After all, hadn't he been the one to point out that a bunch of cattle didn't care if all he wore were the same Western shirts and jeans day after day? And neither did anyone in town. But all he could think about were the thousands of places in New York City where a man who was dating Gemma Chapman could wear that suit.

"It's just that I know how expensive a stay at Maverick Manor is."

"I think I can afford it," he reassured her as he signed for the purchases. "And while we're here, I might as well get that haircut I've been putting off."

He had put his foot down at Janie's idea of him going to some place called Tres Chic and instead took a walk-in appointment at Snip and Style. Afterward he posed for a ridiculous amount of selfies and photos. Both Gemma and Janie finally gave up once he refused to look at the camera with a straight face.

"Okay," Gemma sighed, "I think we have enough pictures of you with your eyes crossed."

"Finally," he said with an eye roll that would have done Janie proud.

They grabbed a quick dinner at the food court, with Janie going for her favorite teriyaki rice bowl, while he had a huge slice of pepperoni pizza and Gemma ate a salad.

"Salad for dinner." Hank shook his head as he took a big bite of the crisp crust with its wonderfully melted cheese and spicy pepperoni. "That is no way to live, Gemma Chapman."

"Um, it actually might be a longer way to live, cowboy," she said as she stabbed a juicy cherry tomato. "Oh, excuse me, rancher."

Their teasing set Janie off into a girlish fit of giggles, while he and Gemma shared a smile. Finished with her meal faster than the adults, his daughter had turned her attention back to the phone. "Look at this one!"

She stuck the cell phone in his face, giving him little choice but to look at it, though he had to hold the small screen back an arm's length before he could focus on the image. It was a selfie of the three of them, and the light and laughter in Janie's face wrapped around his heart the same way her tiny fingers had wrapped around his thumb the very first time he held her. "That's a good one, Janie."

After Janie grabbed her empty bowl and tray and headed for the trash can, Gemma leaned in for a better view of the photo. "I can't say whether or not Janie looks like her aunt Bella, but I can tell you that she looks like one happy girl."

Hank had to agree. He saw how happy Janie looked. But more than that, he saw how happy *he* looked. He swallowed against a lump that felt like half of the pizza crust had lodged in his throat. In this photo, unlike his daughter, he wasn't mugging for the camera. No, he was looking down at Gemma, who was tucked underneath his arm so they could all be in the close-up shot.

He tore his gaze away from the screen as she adjusted the folded cuff of his shirt. Her green-eyed gaze was tender and encouraging as she said, "What you wear isn't so much about how you look but about how you feel."

How he felt? Hank wasn't sure he should spend too much time thinking about how he felt. Especially not after looking at that picture. A picture that proved the shirt on his back had little to do with the smile on his face. No, that was all thanks to the woman on his arm.

"Hank?"

He reluctantly glanced away from Gemma as a female voice called out his name. He spotted Missy Denbrough across the crowded tables. The buxom blonde smiled as she wove her way through the busy food court. "Hank Harlow! I thought that was you, but I couldn't imagine what you'd be doing at the mall in the middle of the week. Or anytime really!"

Hank felt his face flush and wished she hadn't made it sound like he was some kind of hermit, never leaving the ranch except to make a random visit to Rust Creek Falls. Oh, who was he kidding? That was exactly who he was and something Gemma already knew. "I'm here with my daughter."

Missy barely glanced toward Janie, who'd gotten in line for a refill at the soda fountain, her focus locked on him and Gemma to the point where he didn't know how to avoid an introduction. "Gemma Chapman, this is Missy Denbrough. Missy and her family own a ranch outside of Kalispell."

"The Double D," Missy announced proudly before sizing Gemma up with a glance. "I don't think I've seen you around before."

"Gemma's here on vacation. From New York," he added, although he wasn't sure why. Missy didn't need that information, so maybe it was more a way to remind himself.

Missy's smile brightened. "Montana must be such a change for you. I can't even imagine what living in New York is like—all those restaurants and shops and theaters. Life around here must seem so boring in comparison."

"I can't say that I've been bored." She slid a smile in Hank's direction. "Must be the company."

Missy laughed. "Well, sure, it's easy to say that now,

but just wait until there's some freak August storm and you're snowed in by six-foot drifts with no cell service. But, well, you don't have to worry about that, do you? You'll be long gone by then."

Even as Gemma had done her part to transform the ruggedly handsome rancher—to help shake the rust off— she had known some other woman would be the one to claim the polished version of Hank Harlow.

She simply hadn't expected it to happen right in front of her.

As Hank and Missy discussed the price of beef, alfalfa crops and immunizations, echoes of her conversations with Hank from that afternoon bounced around in Gemma's head. Talk about men's fashion and which type of shirt could be worn untucked. The differences between pure cotton and a polyblend. The best colors to make his blue eyes pop.

A shopping spree wasn't going to solve anyone's problems, but as they'd messed around with the camera, posing for pictures, Gemma truly believed that she'd seen an added confidence, as Janie held her head higher and stood a little straighter. And Hank had been such a good sport about adding to his own wardrobe and getting a haircut.

Gemma had felt like she'd made a difference, but now all of it felt so *frivolous*.

She could spot a deal on a pair of Jimmy Choos from a mall away, but the price of beef? The cost of alfalfa? She didn't have a clue when it came to the things that really mattered in Hank's life.

You don't have to know, Gemma reminded herself. *You're only here on vacation.*

Something Hank had been quick to point out to Missy "Double D" Denbrough. Gemma shoved the thought from her mind as she managed to make a proper response when Missy said her farewell.

"So, she seems nice," Gemma murmured.

"She is. Missy knows her stuff. She's been born and raised around cattle ranching her whole life."

All of which made the other woman perfect for Hank.

"Have the two of you ever…?" She let the question trail off, but Hank simply waited, eyebrows raised, as a tension-filled silence lengthened and an embarrassed flush of heat rose to her face.

"Have we ever…what?" he finally asked, the glint in his eyes telling her he knew exactly what she was try-ing not to ask.

"Dated? Have you ever dated?" she demanded, hear-ing a mix of annoyance, frustration and jealousy.

"No, we haven't."

"Sounds like you'd have a lot in common."

"We'd have *ranching* in common."

"And you love ranching."

"I do," Hank agreed, "but sometimes I think I love it too much. Dating a woman like Missy would be like… Well, it would be like dating Carl, the Bar H foreman."

Gemma burst out laughing. "I hope you don't plan on telling Missy that."

"Naw," he said with a grin that sent an arrow straight to Gemma's heart. "Don't plan on tellin' Carl either."

She might not know ranching, but shopping wasn't the only thing she was good at. "You know, the other night at the Ace, Natalie and I were talking about her plan for the future."

"Yeah, and what is her plan this week?"

"She didn't really go into specifics, only that whatever it is, it's going to be big."

Hank chuckled. "That sounds like Nat."

"Well, anyway, I offered to take a look at her finances while I'm here."

Was it her imagination or had Hank's jaw tightened a bit?

"I'm sure Nat appreciates that. I guess you're probably missing work right about now."

Startled, Gemma realized she hadn't missed her job—or New York—at all. "I wish I had the chance to work with people like Natalie. But Carlston, Landry and Greer is more about helping the rich get richer. Not that I should complain. It's certainly a lucrative job, and one I'm good at. Good enough that I might even get the promotion I'm up for."

This time she was sure she hadn't imagined the muscle tightening in Hank's strong jaw. Treading carefully, she said, "But I'd be more than happy if you'd like me to take a look at some of your investments."

"Mine?"

Gemma heard the surprise in Hank's voice and rushed to explain. "You know, like with Natalie. Just to help out and see if there's any place you might be able to set some extra money aside."

"Extra money," he echoed.

"Yes. Janie told me how long it's been since you were able to go on a vacation, and you just said how you were worried the ranch was becoming your whole life. Maybe it would be a good thing if you could, you know, afford to get away more often."

Maybe even to come to New York. The wistful thought whispered through her mind, bringing an added heat to her cheeks as he stared at her with an enigmatic expression. "Or get a new truck one day."

"You don't like my truck?" Hank leaned back in the

chair, a smile playing around his lips. Well, she'd rather amuse him than offend him.

Flustered, Gemma hedged, "It's not that I don't like it. It's just—"

Putting her out of her misery, Hank leaned forward and covered her hands with his own. "I appreciate the offer, Gemma. I do. But you don't have to worry about me. I'm good."

His hands were so big, they completely engulfed hers. They told the story of who he was—strong, capable, hardworking. A gentle squeeze had her lifting her eyes to his. "But what you did today for Janie, that means more to me than all the money in the world."

Gemma wished he would let her do more but figured she was no match for a stubborn rancher's pride. Giving a big sigh, she teased, "Well, I guess it's safe to say you don't want me for my mind?"

Hank gave a laugh. "Sweetheart, even a dumb cowboy knows there's no good answer to that question...except maybe to say that I want *you*, Gemma Chapman. Each and every part of you."

No good answer? Then how was it he'd found the one guaranteed to make her heart melt?

The following night, Gemma stopped short as Hank tried to guide her down one of the back paths leading from the hotel. Crossing her arms over her chest, she demanded, "Why exactly do you want me to trek through the Montana wilderness in the middle of the night?"

Hank laughed. "Even I wouldn't call eight thirty the middle of the night. And aren't you the one from the City That Never Sleeps? Besides, it's not like I'm taking you out into Glacier National Park and throwing you to the wolves," Hank argued.

"There are wolves?"

He caught her hand when she pretended to dash back inside where the warmth and glow of the Manor's gleaming chandelier beckoned. "Forget the wolves."

"Easy for you to say," she muttered while trying to hide a smile.

"Hey, if anyone should be worried about wolves, it's me. Wolves dressed in trendy teenage-boy clothing," he muttered. He wasn't entirely sure he was kidding, but the sound of Gemma's laughter settled into his heart, making him feel lighter and younger.

They'd spent the day by the pool, and this time he and Janie had convinced Gemma to do more than relax in one of the loungers. She'd surprised them both by doing a cannonball into the deep end, unconcerned about her hair or her makeup or even the fact that she could barely swim—something Hank realized a moment later as she came up sputtering and struggling to tread water.

"What were you thinking?" he'd demanded as he pulled her toward the steps.

Pushing her dark locks from her face, she'd grinned at him. "That I'm done living life in the shallow end!"

Shaking his head, he'd told her, "You might want to learn to swim first."

But she'd only lifted a challenging eyebrow. "No time like the present."

After dinner at Maverick Manor's dining room, the three of them had played a few of the old-fashioned board games in the lobby. Dan had been teaching Janie to play chess, and she could now beat Hank hands down. But it was the confidence in Janie's expression as she scooted her chair closer to the board to explain all of the moves to Gemma that Hank enjoyed the most.

"It's been years since I've played," Gemma had confessed, "and even then, I barely knew the rules. I'm pretty sure the only thing I remember for sure is that the queen has all the best moves."

"Isn't that the truth," Hank murmured, earning a wink from Gemma over Janie's head.

They'd played for half an hour or so before a group of girls a bit older than Janie walked by the fireplace. A tall brunette flicked her long hair over one shoulder as she spoke. "Board games are so lame."

The others, clearly following the brunette's lead, nodded while a second girl added, "Yeah, they're for babies."

Janie's face reddened and it took everything inside of Hank—and the gentle hand Gemma placed on his arm—to keep from jumping to his daughter's defense. But any comment he made would only further embarrass Janie, and no grown man could have an argument with a bunch of teenage girls and not make a fool of himself.

But he was proud of how Janie had held her head high despite the color in her cheeks. Speaking loudly enough for the girls to overhear, she said, "Gemma, did you know chess is considered the game of kings?"

"My grandpa told me that when he taught me to play."

At the sound of the new voice, the three of them looked up. A young boy with hair long enough to flop over his left eye walked over to the table, his hands stuffed in the pockets of his skinny jeans. "It's a cool game," he added.

The girls who'd been laughing earlier stood with their mouths hanging open, but with nothing to say now.

"Yeah," Janie said shyly. "It is."

"I haven't had anyone to play with since my grandpa moved away."

"Well, why don't you and Janie play?" Gemma had

immediately suggested as she slid her chair over to make room—much to Hank's dismay.

But when Janie turned to him with her eyes bright with hope and asked, "Can we, Dad?" he didn't have time to figure out how to get her back to the Bar H and lock her into her room until she was thirty.

Their well-played matches had ended in a two-two tie, and considering his daughter's competitive streak, Hank had no doubt the kid had beat Janie fair and square. They were setting up for the tiebreaker when one of the hotel employees stopped by to tell them about another movie night organized for all the teen and preteen guests at the hotel—this time a feature of the most recent super-hero flick.

Once again Hank hadn't figured out how to say no.

But that didn't stop him from asking Gemma now, "And what kind of a name is Bennett anyway?"

Smothering a laugh, she said, "A perfectly nice name for what I am sure is a perfectly nice boy."

As Hank grumbled, Gemma added, "And I'm not sure you have a boot to stand on, Hank Harlow, worrying about boys flirting with girls…not when you just asked me to take a walk with you in the woods!"

"Good point. I'm not letting Janie date until she's at least forty-seven."

Gemma laughed again, but she tucked her hand in the crook of his arm as if they were attending some fancy ball. "It's not when you date, Hank," she told him. "It's who. And with you as an example, she'll know the kind of man she should look for."

With the full moon overhead, Hank could read the wistful expression on Gemma's face. A kind of *what if* that must have followed her her whole life as she wondered about the father she never had the chance to know.

She might have come to Montana nursing a bruised heart from a broken engagement, but she'd been looking for more than a Wild West vacation. The chance to go horseback riding or to learn the two-step wouldn't be enough to supply the missing pieces from her life. He had an idea of what might help, but that would have to wait until he could make some calls first. For now he could at least show her a Rust Creek Falls experience that was not to be missed.

"What is this?" Gemma asked as Hank led the way toward a moonlit clearing and a romantic picnic—complete with a red-and-black checkered blanket, a wicker basket and a small lantern adding a soft glow.

"You mentioned something about sleeping under the stars. And while I should tell you that spending the night on the hard ground isn't nearly as glamorous as it sounds, I thought we could at least enjoy a moonlit picnic."

"Hank, this is amazing."

Hank gave a small laugh as they settled onto the blanket. "I have to give Maverick Manor credit for pulling out all the stops for its guests. All I had to do was mention wanting to go on a picnic, and the staff had this ready."

"The staff didn't plan this. That was all you. So, what's in our picnic?"

"Hot chocolate and marshmallows." Even as he pulled the thermos and bag of sugary treats from the basket, he recalled the elegant and romantic display room service had delivered to Gemma's room that first night. Heat climbed up his neck as he said, "It's not exactly champagne and oysters."

"Thank goodness! I hate oysters."

"Yeah," Hank said with a smile. "Well, this basket is shellfish free."

It turned out, though, that it was not romance free. Had he really thought marshmallows childish? He clearly hadn't taken into consideration the ambience of the flickering flames from the small fire he had built. Or the way Gemma cupped the hot chocolate between her hands, breathing in the rich, fragrant steam with her eyes closed, a look of pure rapture on her face. And he certainly hadn't counted on the sheer seduction of feeding her a perfectly roasted golden marshmallow and the mind-blowing experience of her licking the sticky, sweet treat from his fingers.

The knowing look in her eyes told him she was aware of exactly what she was doing to him, and with a low growl he caught her face in his hands and it was his turn to taste the flame-roasted marshmallow—right from Gemma's lips.

Her mouth opened beneath his, and the combination of chocolate, marshmallow and Gemma ruined his sweet tooth for life. Nothing—nothing—would ever taste so decadent, so addicting, for the rest of his life.

The blood pounding through his veins felt thick and molten as he followed Gemma down on the checkered blanket. Her body was soft and supple beneath his own, her breasts pressing against his chest, her legs parting for his hips. She ran her hands through his hair, and he suddenly regretted getting it cut too short for her to fist her hands into.

He didn't have that problem. Gemma's long locks surrounded him as he rolled onto his back until the weight and warmth of her body draped over him, her hair forming a curtain as dark and mysterious as the night around them.

She gasped his name as he reached between them, his hands cupping her breasts through the thin sweater and bra, clothes separating them the last thing he wanted. He wanted nothing to separate them. Nothing.

But while the small meadow was off the beaten path, it was not entirely secluded. And what he'd said about sleeping on the hard ground went double for making love. He slid his hands to the slightly less seductive curve of Gemma's hips as he murmured her name against her lips.

He gentled the kiss as he rolled them to their sides. He could see the flickering firelight reflected in Gemma's eyes, and he'd never wanted a woman more. But he wanted complete privacy and total luxury—exactly like what Maverick Manor's honeymoon suite offered.

"Janie and I are checking out of the hotel tomorrow. Anne and Dan will be coming by to pick her up." His voice was rough to his own ears with desire and something he refused to define. The week he'd expected to drag on had skipped by in a heartbeat since he'd met Gemma, and now every dull thud in his chest seemed to count down the moments until her time in Rust Creek Falls was over.

"Time to go back to real life," Gemma whispered, an echo of the words he'd spoken the first day they met.

But if the excitement and anticipation thrumming through his veins every time they were together wasn't real, then how was it Hank felt more alive these past seven days than he had in the past seven years?

"I suppose you have to get back to the Bar H."

For a brief second, Hank thought about taking the easy way out. Of cutting ties before he got in too deep. But as Gemma gazed at him—the longing and loneliness in his own heart reflected in her eyes—he couldn't do it. The desire, the need to spend whatever time he could with her, was too great, and he wondered if it wasn't already too late when instead of letting go, he wanted to reach out and hold on.

"Not tomorrow." He watched as her eyes lit as he added, "I want to spend tomorrow with you."

Chapter Nine

"I don't wanna go home."

Despite all her claims that she was grown-up, Janie could still put on a childish pout when the occasion fit. And standing in the Maverick Manor lobby with their suitcases at their sides, boy, did this occasion fit. But one of them needed to be the grown-up in the situation, and Hank figured it had to be him.

Even though he didn't want to leave either.

It's not goodbye, he reminded himself. Anne and Dan were picking up Janie from the hotel, but Hank wasn't heading back to the Bar H. Not yet. He and Gemma had already made plans to spend the afternoon together, and he was a little nervous about how she would react to what he had in mind.

"Janie, we were here on vacation, and our reservation ends today. You know your mom and Dan have been missing you. She has all kinds of things planned for you, not to mention the two new puppies you'll be taking care of."

Anne had sent her daughter a text the day before. A litter of adorable mutts had been abandoned at the veterinarian clinic where Anne worked. Because the dogs were too young to be put up for adoption, the staff had all agreed to foster them until they were old enough to go to permanent homes. Anne and Dan had taken in a male and a female, and Janie was already thinking of names. Hank wouldn't be surprised if the two pups ended up as permanent members of the family.

Janie's pout lifted slightly. "The pictures of the puppies Mom sent are so cute! But…just because I go home doesn't mean you couldn't stay… You know, with Gemma."

Stay at Maverick Manor with Gemma…

Hank knew his daughter didn't mean that the way it sounded, but images of following Gemma into the honeymoon suite and following her down onto the enormous four-poster bed left him light-headed.

After last night's kiss under the stars, Hank thought—hoped—their relationship might be headed in that direction. But he wanted Gemma to be sure. For all her brash city-girl talk, more than once Hank had caught a glimpse of the lost-and-lonely girl beneath the high-fashion exterior. The lost-and-lonely *cowgirl* who'd come to Rust Creek Falls because it was the place her father had once called home.

Seeming to take his silence as a sign that he was weakening, Janie pressed her point. "Gemma will be here all by herself, and for a whole nother week," she added as if that was an eternity. And maybe to someone her age it was. But Hank knew that the time would pass in a blink, and then Gemma would be the one to say goodbye.

"Look! There she is!" As Janie rushed across the

crowded lobby, Hank forced himself to follow at a slower pace. His daughter gave her a tight hug, and he could hear the tears in her voice as she said, "This has been the best vacation ever!"

"For me, too. I'm so glad I had the chance to meet you. And remember, this isn't goodbye. You already have my cell number, and we'll video chat once I'm back home."

Hank knew Gemma's heart was in the right place, but he figured that would change once she got back to New York, back to her real life. He had a hard time imagining a gorgeous woman like Gemma staying at home to video chat with his daughter when she could be out on the town, enjoying all the big city had to offer.

And as for him, he would not be calling Gemma's cell or video chatting once she left. Those faint and distant connections would never be enough. Not when he wanted so much more.

Gemma waved back at Janie as Anne and Dan pulled out of Maverick Manor's parking lot. "That is one amazing girl you have there, Hank Harlow." She wasn't surprised to feel the ache of tears in her throat as she tried to swallow. Janie had made her way into Gemma's heart with her bright smile and sheer exuberance. And if watching the young girl drive away had been hard, Gemma could only imagine the heartache in store when the time came to say goodbye to Hank.

"Yeah," he said, his own voice sounding a little rough. "She's a great kid. And she's never going to forget this vacation. I want to thank you for being such a big part of it."

"It was my pleasure." As much as she enjoyed sharing Hank with Janie during their time at Maverick Manor, she was glad to know she would at least have him all to herself today. "So, what do you have planned for this afternoon?"

"There are some people I'd like you to meet," he told her as he led her toward his truck.

Gemma blinked. "Oh." His words were so much the opposite of what she had been thinking, she wasn't sure what to say.

"I've been thinking about that list of yours. It's all about things you would have learned to do if you'd been brought up here, isn't it? If you'd been raised as a cowgirl."

If you'd known your father.

Hank didn't say the words, but she could read them in the compassion in his gaze.

"I'd always wondered what if," she confessed. "What if he hadn't been killed when I was so young? What if he hadn't walked out on my mother when she was pregnant? And then I found out that wasn't even true. My mother lied. My father *was* a part of my life during those first years. It's just a part I wasn't old enough to remember."

"Oh, Gem, sweetheart."

"When I discovered he was from Rust Creek Falls, I wanted to come here. To try to imagine what life might have been like..."

From the hilltop location, Gemma had a perfect view of the town. At that distance, Rust Creek Falls looked postcard perfect—the place that had lived in her imagination since she first saw the name as her father's place of birth. Now that she'd been there, she knew it wasn't perfect. It was real. Filled with real people with real problems. The sense of community, the small charm, that was real, too.

"I can't give you back those memories, Gemma, but maybe I can give you the next best thing."

"I don't understand."

"I made some calls this morning. You remember Melba Strickland? The woman who owns the boarding-house in town?"

"The one who thought she recognized me? Yes, I remember, but what—"

"The Stricklands have lived here for decades, and they know just about everyone in town."

Gemma swallowed against a dry throat as she realized what Hank was saying. "Did they—did they know my father?"

"They recognized his name. They're pretty sure his father, your grandfather, was a ranch hand for the Traubs. The Triple T has been in their family for generations. Ellie and Bob Traub are a big part of the community."

"You shouldn't have. I didn't ask you to do this, Hank." Faced with the idea of discovering something more about her father than a faded thirty-year-old photograph, she felt her heart start racing. And suddenly she wanted to run the thousands of miles back to New York. "You had no right!"

"Gemma."

He reached for her, but she backed away from his touch.

"What are you afraid of?"

"I am not afraid!" So why was sheer terror filling her lungs and making it almost impossible to breathe? What if the pictures were the lie and what her mother had told her was the truth? What if her father had walked out of Gemma's life, leaving her behind, only a few years later than when her mother had told her?

"No, not the girl who was ready to jump on a horse even though she doesn't know how to ride. Not the girl who dove into the deep end of the pool even though she doesn't know how to swim. Not the girl who said to hell with what anyone thinks and went on a honeymoon for one. No, that girl isn't afraid of anything."

Tears burned her eyes as she whispered, "What if I'm really not that girl?"

This time when Hank reached out, she went willingly into his arms. With her cheek pressed to his chest, she could hear the sure, steady pounding of his heartbeat. She breathed in the clean scent of fabric softener and soap as he held her tightly. Even though Gemma knew it wasn't possible, she felt as though the simple connection had somehow imbued her with his confidence, his strength, his simple certainty in knowing who he was and where he belonged.

"That is exactly who you are. You might be a city girl on the outside, but on the inside you have the heart of a cowgirl. Don't ever doubt it. And remember, no matter what we find out from the Traubs, it doesn't change who you are…or who you still can be."

It doesn't change who you are…or who you still can be.

Gemma clung to Hank's words as his truck bumped along the road toward the Traub ranch. When she'd asked if they should call first, he'd reassured her that neighbors dropped in on neighbors all the time, and anyone who lived in Rust Creek Falls was considered a neighbor.

As if reading the nerves shaking her from head to toe, Hank reached over, entwined her fingers with his and drew her arm over so the back of her hand pressed against the solid muscle of his thigh.

"It's gonna be okay," he reassured her.

It doesn't change who you are…

As he drove toward the ranch house, he filled her in on the elder Traubs and their six sons.

"It's been so long since my father would have lived

here. Do you really think the Traubs will remember him?" Gemma asked him.

"One thing I've learned about small towns is that they have long memories. In fact, if your grandfather was a hand for the Traub ranch and if your father actually grew up here, then you'll find yourself right in the middle of the Traub-Crawford feud."

Enough teasing filled Hank's voice that Gemma didn't dare take him seriously. "There's a feud?"

"Yep. One going back for generations. Although Natalie's sister, Nina, did a lot to defuse the whole thing when she and the Traubs' eldest son, Dallas, got married some years ago."

"I bet that makes for an interesting holiday get-together."

Hank's low chuckle filled not just the interior of the cab but Gemma's entire being. As he pulled up in front of a sprawling ranch house, he asked, "Are you ready for this?"

Hank had stoked her curiosity about the Traubs and the feud and, most of all, her father's possible connection to them, so she couldn't turn away. But that didn't stop her knees from shaking a few moments later as Hank knocked on the front door.

A sixtysomething woman opened the door, a smile lighting her round face when she caught sight of Hank. "Hank, this is a surprise."

"Hi, Ellie. I hope we're not interrupting."

"Of course not! Our door is always open to our friends and neighbors." The woman's expression was warm and welcoming, but Gemma didn't miss the curiosity in her gaze.

"This is Gemma Chapman. She's visiting Rust Creek Falls, but it turns out she might have a connection to the town and to your ranch."

Ellie's eyebrow rose. "Well, doesn't that sound mysterious? Why don't you come on in? If you have questions about the ranch, my husband will be the one with the answers."

As Ellie ushered them into the living room, Gemma glanced at the mantel and the multitude of framed photos. No doubt the handsome cowboys on display were the six Traub brothers and their happy, growing families.

"Give me just a moment to call my husband in from the backyard. He's out there, manning the grill."

Just then Gemma caught a whiff of the mouthwatering scents drifting in from the kitchen, a mix of freshly baked bread and something with a hint of smoky, spicy flavors. "We're interrupting—"

"Not at all," Ellie reassured her with a wave of her hand. "Around here, it's always the more the merrier. Please, have a seat."

Though Gemma was sure the oversize leather couch was perfectly comfortable, she might as well have been sitting on pins and needles.

"Relax," Hank encouraged her.

"Nothing I find out will change who I am," she echoed.

"That's right," he reassured her. "And who you are is pretty amazing."

Who she was was a single city girl with a career and an apartment waiting for her back in New York City. *What about who I can be?*

Gemma didn't have a chance to ask Hank that question before an older man stepped into the living room with Ellie at his side. He greeted Hank with a handshake before turning to Gemma with the tip of his worn cowboy hat.

"Bob, this is Gemma Chapman," Ellie said by way of introduction, "and Hank thinks she might have a connection to the ranch."

Given that explanation, Gemma expected some kind

of suspicion or distrust to enter the older man's gaze, but instead she saw nothing but curiosity. "Really? Well, this ranch has a history that goes back for more years than you've been alive, Ms. Chapman. So anything is possible."

Nothing will change who you can be... Anything is possible...

Gemma wasn't sure which she wanted to believe more, but Hank was right. She needed to know the truth. "My father's name was Daryl Reems, and Mrs. Strickland seemed to think his father might have worked here years ago."

"Daryl Reems..."

Holding her breath, she waited, bracing herself for disappointment.

Sorry, I don't recognize the name.

Reems, you say? Sounds vaguely familiar, but I don't really remember...

Instead an almost wistful note entered Bob Traub's voice as he confessed, "I haven't heard that name in almost thirty years."

Her heart in her throat, Gemma asked, "You knew my father?"

"Knew him?" Bob gave a husky laugh. "The two of us practically grew up together. He was like a brother to me." He shook off the memories, and his gaze sharpened as he focused on Gemma. "So, you're Daryl's daughter... His precious gem."

"His...what?"

"That's what Daryl always called you. His precious gem."

A few hours later, Hank could see how the emotional day was taking a toll on Gemma. Not that Ellie and Bob

Traub were anything other than kind and compassionate as they told tales about Gemma's father growing up on the ranch. They had welcomed Gemma with open arms—as did their sons as they arrived one after another, along with their wives and children, for the Traub Saturday afternoon barbecue.

The elder Traubs had insisted Hank and Gemma stay, with Ellie waving aside their protests about imposing and laughing at the idea that there might not be enough food as Bob added yet another leaf to the table. "One thing this family is never short of, and that's food." Reaching out, the older woman gave Gemma a quick hug. "There's always more than enough to go round."

Tears had welled up in Gemma's eyes at the older woman's warm embrace, and Hank had been glad when Collin Traub, former bad boy turned good and the current mayor of Rust Creek Falls, chimed in from his seat across from Gemma. "So, now that you're practically family, has anyone filled you in on the Traub-Crawford feud?"

A few groans sounded from around the enormous dinner table, where the adults had gathered, and Hank shot Gemma a wink. Collin shook his head in mock gravity. "From what I hear, you and Natalie have been hanging out, but you've gotta put an end to that."

Gemma's startled look turned to laughter as Collin's younger brother Dallas lobbed a roll at his brother's head.

"Children," Ellie admonished from the head of the table.

"What?" Collin demanded as he tore the roll in half and slathered it with butter. "Hating the Crawfords is a deep-seated Traub family tradition!"

"I resent that remark," Nina Crawford Traub said mildly before she leaned over to kiss her husband, Dallas, causing a second round of groans.

Collin shook his head in dismay. "I'm telling you, we had a good thing going around here until these two had to go all Romeo and Juliet on us."

"What can I say?" Dallas asked. "True love conquers all."

True love...

The words were still ringing in Hank's ears an hour later as he and Gemma said their goodbyes. He wrapped his arm around her shoulders, and she nestled her head against his shoulder. Despite the Traubs' warm hospitality throughout the evening, Gemma hadn't once left his side. Or was it that he hadn't left hers?

He wished he could believe that Dallas was right. After all, true love had bridged a feud spanning almost a hundred years. Was it possible it could erase a distance of two thousand or so miles?

Gemma's shoulders tensed slightly as Bob Traub pulled her into his arms only to practically melt into his embrace as he gruffly said, "Your daddy would be so proud of the smart, beautiful woman you've become."

Hank had to give her credit for holding herself together. Even though her long lashes were fluttering faster than a hummingbird's wings, she kept up her smile until they made it out the front door and down to his truck. As he opened the passenger door, she let out a sudden sob and covered her mouth with her hand.

"Oh, sweetheart," he murmured as he wrapped his arms around her and cradled her to his chest. He pressed a kiss to the top of her head, much as Bob Traub had a moment ago, though Hank's feelings were far from fatherly. But they were protective—an instinct to battle Gemma's demons and guard her against all harm. He only hoped to hell he wasn't the one who had harmed her.

"I am so sorry," he murmured. "I thought it might help you to find some people who had known your father. I didn't think…" He cut off a brief curse. "I didn't stop to think about how hard it was going to be for you to deal with all you'd lost."

"Lost?" she echoed on a watery laugh. "Oh, Hank."

As she pulled back far enough to look up at him with eyes glistening like the forest after a summer rain, she said, "I'm not crying because I'm sad. Hearing all those stories about my father from people who loved him, people who considered him family and welcomed me the same way… That means so much to me. And it was all thanks to you."

She pressed her fingertips to his lips when he would have argued. "Your faith in me gave me the strength to believe I can be whoever I want to be."

And when she rose up to kiss him, Hank swore he could taste the change in her. She was no longer the city girl looking to escape her broken engagement, nor the wannabe cowgirl searching for a piece of her past, but someone new. Someone with the confidence to choose a bigger, brighter path.

Pulling her body tightly to his, he could only thank his lucky stars that she had chosen him.

He'd given her a miracle.

That was the thought that kept circling through Gemma's mind as they drove back to Maverick Manor. The sun was starting to sink behind the mountains, vivid pinks and purples and oranges streaking across the western sky. Hank had cracked the windows to let in the cool, pine-scented evening air, and he glanced over when a small shiver streaked down her spine. "Do you want me to roll up the window?"

"No, I'm fine." The breeze ruffled through his thick hair the way Gemma's fingers itched to do, and it wasn't the cold that had goose bumps rushing across her skin.

It was Hank. His kindness, his caring… She gazed at his handsome profile, backlit by the setting sun, and could barely swallow around the lump in her throat. His…*everything.*

He'd given her such a precious gift—something she'd never had before. Memories of her father. That they were shared memories of people who had known him, people who had loved him, didn't dilute the images in Gemma's mind. If anything, they were even more vivid, even more powerful, as they gave her deeper, stronger ties to Rust Creek Falls and the friends and the *family* she had met.

Maybe she was getting greedy, but Gemma didn't want her memories of Rust Creek Falls to end there. She didn't want them to end at all. She knew Hank felt the same when instead of turning into the visitor's parking lot, he drove right up to the front of Maverick Manor and handed the valet the keys. She wasn't sure how they made it to the room, stopping to kiss every few feet beneath the golden glow of old-fashioned sconces in the long hallway leading to the suite.

As Gemma reached up to run her lips along the underside of his strong jaw, Hank fumbled with the key card. He cursed, making her laugh, as it took two tries for him to get the card into the slot. "Oh, you think it's funny, do you?" he all but growled.

"Well, you did say you were rusty—" Her words ended in a shriek as he picked her up and flung her over his shoulder as if she were weightless. The wild, upside-down ride ended with Gemma giggling and landing with a breathless bounce as he tossed her into the middle of the wide white canopy bed.

As he followed her down on the soft mattress, her laughter faded away. He was still and quiet above her before he brushed a strand of hair away from her cheek with an aching tenderness. His body lay full-length alongside hers. All hard muscle and long, masculine limbs. Shoulder to shoulder, breast to chest, thigh to thigh...

The temptation was so... Hank. The combination of strength and gentleness that she could never resist. Was she really surprised she'd fallen in love with him? Of course she had. How could she not?

"Are you sure about this, Gemma?"

She'd never been more certain of anything in her life. Just like finding those old photos had been like finding a piece of her past, loving Hank was like finding the other half of her heart. The words rose in the back of her throat, but she silenced them quickly. Too soon, too much... But he was waiting for her answer, unwilling to assume, refusing to push.

Just waiting. For her. Like she had been waiting for him her whole life.

"Oh, Hank, yes."

Like lighting a fuse, Gemma felt as though she had set him on fire with those words. His blue eyes blazed as his strong fingers went to his shirt. At first she thought he'd ripped it clean open until she discovered the absolute joy of snap-front Western wear. Her hands were on his naked skin in seconds, the light covering of chest hair tickling her palms as she discovered the hard planes and jaw-dropping six-pack.

She pushed the soft cotton from his shoulders as his hands moved to the tiny buttons of her shirt. Unlike with his own clothes, he took his time, sliding each pearl through the hole until Gemma thought she might go crazy. Finally, finally he pulled the panels apart to reveal her black bra.

His grin had her pulse pounding through her veins. "You might be a cowgirl at heart, but this—" he ran a finger over the lace edge of the cups "—this is all city girl underneath."

"Don't be so sure about that, cowboy," she warned, and she pulled a stunt that would have made a steer wrestler proud as she shoved Hank onto his back and straddled him. "I've learned some moves in Montana."

She swallowed his rough laugh with her kiss as she bent over him. He buried his hands in her hair, holding her to him, even as his tongue delved deeper. His hands found her breasts as he brushed the bra aside, and Gemma could feel her body softening, melting like the delicious, decadent marshmallows they had roasted under the starlit Montana sky.

But those billions of stars had nothing on the galaxy of color and light and emotion shooting through Gemma as Hank stripped the rest of her clothes away and came back to her naked and ready. Her body opened for him in an instant, their joining so right, so perfect that she couldn't hold back.

"Gemma. Gemma." The words dropped from his lips only to be caught by hers in an endless kiss. The taste, the texture, the sheer amazement of holding Hank in her arms could have gone on forever.

Too much…and yet never enough.

The pressure built inside her, as overwhelming and intense as she'd ever imagined. And then pleasure burst like a meteor shower, raining down over them as he called out her name.

Gemma wasn't sure what she expected the next morning, but it wasn't waking up in the honeymoon suite alone. She told herself that Hank wasn't on vacation any longer. His reservation had ended the day before, and he was expected back at the ranch. All of which made perfect sense to her head, if not to her heart.

Her heart was still vulnerable enough to wonder if last night hadn't meant as much to Hank as it had to her. If she didn't mean as much.

Gemma tossed the sheets aside, determined to do the same with her worries. She'd trusted Hank last night enough to fall asleep in his arms. She would trust him even now that she hadn't had the chance to wake up in them this morning.

As she slid on the robe that was draped over the foot of the bed, a faint buzz had her hands tightening on the sash. The sound of her phone vibrating inside her purse. Much as it had all afternoon yesterday while she and Hank listened to stories about the father Gemma had never known.

A father who had loved her. A father who had wanted to be a part of her life. A father who was a hardworking, honest, respectable man. A father her mother had lied to Gemma about for thirty years.

"Hello, Mother."

"Well, it is about time," Diane Chapman stated once Gemma answered the phone. "I was starting to think they didn't even have cell service in that place."

"Is that why you were calling? To check on phone reception in Montana?"

"Of course not. I was hoping you'd come to your senses. You've already been gone over a week. You should come home. This is hardly a time to be away from the firm— especially with the promotion on the line."

"Nothing's been decided yet," Gemma argued, but her mother's silence on the other end made her wonder if perhaps a decision had been made—thanks to her

.stepfather's influence. Gemma's hand tightened on the phone. "I'm staying in Montana, Mother."

"What?"

"Until the end of my reservation. I'm staying until the end of my reservation."

But despite the added explanation, the words echoed through the honeymoon suite. *I'm staying...*

"I don't have any idea why you wanted to go there in the first place."

"Don't you?" Gemma pressed. "You never even asked where in Montana I was staying."

"Because you told me... Some manor place."

"Maverick Manor. In Rust Creek Falls."

Even across the cell phone connection, Gemma heard her mother's sharp inhalation. "Rust Creek—why, Gemma? What do you expect to find there?"

"Maybe some answers? Some piece of my life, some piece of *myself*, that's been missing all of these years."

"Your life is in New York," Diane insisted. "Anything that's missing, anything that you are searching for, you'll find it here. Not in that place."

She heard the scorn that practically dripped from her mother's voice. "Why are you so sure that I'd hate it here?"

"Because I did!"

"You..." Gemma sank down onto the bed as she suddenly remembered Melba Strickland's words. *I never forget a face...* And everyone said how much Gemma resembled her mother. "You came to Rust Creek Falls? You stayed at Strickland's Boarding House?"

After a long moment, Diane stated, "I checked into some creaky old inn. I don't remember what it was called."

"When was this?"

"After I realized I was pregnant," her mother told her. "I went to Rust Creek Falls and stayed a few days while

I tried to find your father. Cell phones weren't around back then, so it took me a while to discover he was working on some middle-of-nowhere dirt farm another town over."

Gemma tried to imagine her mother living somewhere outside of New York and couldn't even picture it. Least of all in Montana. "You actually lived here?"

"For four months. It was a mistake, but I was young… and foolish."

"I don't understand why you never told me. Why did you let me believe my father simply walked out on you?"

"By the time you were old enough to ask questions, Daryl had already passed away and I was dating your stepfather. He was going to be the only father you would remember, so why bring up the past? What would have been the point?"

"The point?" she echoed. "Only that I would have known my father didn't abandon me. That he cared about me. That he loved me."

"Gemma," her mother sighed, "I would think by now you would know that love isn't everything. Yes, your father loved you. He even said he loved me. But at the end of those four months, he's the one who told me I should go back home. He didn't love me—love us— enough to ask me to stay."

After being away from the Bar H for over a week, Hank had expected coming home to feel like a relief. He should have walked in, dumped his dirty laundry into the basket, stowed his luggage away in the attic, where it would once again gather dust for the unforeseeable future, and breathed a huge sigh that he was finally home.

Instead the once-comfortable space seemed too big, too…empty. He hadn't felt so alone since Anne and Janie had first moved out, but that was crazy. He'd lived on his own at the Bar H for years now. He was used to being alone. He liked being alone on the ranch, which was his refuge.

So why did every beat of his heart, every breath in his body, urge him to turn right around and head back to Maverick Manor?

To Gemma.

He still wasn't sure how he forced himself out of the bed where Gemma had still been sleeping. She'd been lying on her side, her hands tucked beneath her cheek, her dark hair spread out against the pristine pillowcase.

Never had he been so tempted to forget about the Bar H, about the work and responsibility waiting for him on the ranch, and that alone had spurred him into action.

For far too long, other than his weekends with Janie, the ranch had been all he had. He'd reluctantly agreed to the weeklong vacation with Janie, but only after carefully planning for his absence and only because he would do anything to make her happy. He would do anything to make Gemma happy as well, but not once had she asked him to stay, which only reinforced how desperately he needed to go.

But when he checked in with Carl after he'd spotted the foreman near the stables, he learned everything was running smoothly. Most of his employees had worked for him since the early days of the Bar H, so it was no wonder why the wheels had kept turning. No reason to think the day-to-day operations would grind to a halt just because he'd spent a week in town. No reason to think they wouldn't keep running that way if he were gone a few days more.

"Hey, boss." Carl's boots struck against the concrete

floor of the stables. "Got some fences down in the east pasture. Are you ready to saddle up?"

Settling his hat low on his forehead, he nodded. Ready or not, his vacation was over. "Time to get back to work."

Back to real life.

Chapter Ten

Gemma caught sight of Natalie Crawford waving to her from a back booth of the Gold Rush Diner. The scent of fried food carried over from the kitchen, and the ding of a bell and the call of "Order's up!" filled the air. She'd been looking forward to lunch with the other woman, and that was before the phone call with her mother. With the conversation seeming to echo through every corner of the honeymoon suite, Gemma had showered and dressed quickly in her new Western wardrobe, eager to leave the room.

Not that it helped her escape the thoughts careening through her head. As she'd driven through town, she kept trying to picture her mother there and couldn't. It was like trying to picture the Chrysler Building on the corner of Sawmill Street and Broomtail Road. Gemma wasn't sure which would have stood out more.

Your life is in New York.

Her mother's life certainly was, but was Gemma's? For so long she had followed the path her mother and stepfather had laid out for her. Prep school, college, her job at Carlston, Landry and Greer, and even her relationship with Chad. But were the long workweeks, the superficial relationships and the drive to succeed to prove her worth really living?

It doesn't change who you still can be.

Hank believed that she could be something more, that she deserved something better. His faith in her was enough to do what nothing else had that morning—push her mother's voice from her head and lift her spirits enough for her to greet Natalie with a smile.

"Thanks for meeting me for lunch," Natalie said as Gemma slid across the burgundy faux-leather booth.

"I'm glad you were free." Gemma managed a small laugh. "Sometimes I forget that not everyone is here on vacation."

Natalie wrinkled her nose. "Yeah, I'm scheduled at the store this whole week. I'll probably see if I can pick up some of my sister's shifts, too. Stupid car broke down—again. And the way things are going, it's gonna take me forever to pay for the repairs. Forget ever getting a new car."

From the time Gemma had spent with the other woman, she'd already figured out that Natalie had some big dreams but no real plan on how to see any of them through. "I take it you don't have a savings account."

Natalie rolled her eyes. "I'm more into spending than saving."

"I'm happy to help you set up a budget—one that would allow you to spend, but also to set aside some savings for emergency expenses or even for a down payment on that new car."

"I don't know… Numbers really aren't my thing. I can't even tell you the last time I balanced my checkbook."

The number cruncher in Gemma cringed at the thought, but she insisted, "You don't have to be good with numbers or even that good with money. The easiest thing to do would be to look at where you're spending money, where you might be able to save some, and then set up an account to pull that money directly from your paycheck each week. And don't think of it as a savings account. Think of it as your…new-BMW account."

Natalie snorted. "Yeah, right. Me driving around Rust Creek Falls in a Beemer."

"Okay, so bad vehicle example, but you get my point. If you know what you're saving for, sometimes it's easier to set the money aside."

"I would love one of those new Jeeps that are so cute."

"Okay, so there you go. Natalie's Jeep Fund."

For the next hour or so over a turkey burger and fries, Gemma walked Natalie through her expenses. They came up with a budget that would mean cutting some corners on shopping and going out, but would make buying a new car an obtainable goal rather than some far-off dream.

"Thanks for doing all of this," Natalie said as they finished up their meal. She handed over her credit card to the waitress. "My treat as a thank-you for your hard work… and because it will probably be the last time I'll be eating out for a while."

"I'm afraid that's true," she admitted. "And about all those credit cards…"

Natalie groaned. "Enough about me and my poor credit karma. I'd rather hear about you striking gold with a guy like Hank Harlow."

"He is kind of incredible," Gemma said softly. She had no doubt her cheeks were turning red, and while she had no intention of telling Natalie just how incredible, Gemma did explain how he'd introduced her to the Traubs and about her father's connection to the Rust Creek Falls family.

"I should have known!" Natalie slapped a hand down on the chipped Formica table. "I should have realized there was a reason why we hit it off so quickly."

"I'm not sure I'm following—you're a Crawford, and considering my father grew up with the Traubs, doesn't that mean we should be mortal enemies?"

"Exactly!" Natalie stressed. "We *should* be."

Given the other woman's wild-child reputation, Gemma gave a small laugh. "Let me guess. You aren't one to do what people think you should."

"Now you're catching on." Lifting what was left of her diet cola, Natalie pronounced, "To the Rust Creek rebels!"

No one had ever called Gemma a rebel. At least not until she'd made up her mind to go on a honeymoon for one. "To the rebels," she echoed as she clinked her glass of iced tea against Natalie's.

"Speaking of which, as grateful as I am for your help, why are you here when you and Hank could be enjoying some of Maverick Manor's finest amenities? Like the enormous bed in the honeymoon suite?"

Gemma took a sip of her watered-down iced tea, fiddling with the straw as she avoided her friend's gaze. "Hank went back to the Bar H. His vacation ended yesterday."

"Yours didn't." Natalie snagged the pen the waitress had left behind and started writing on the back of the receipt.

"What's this?" Gemma asked when her friend handed over the piece of paper.

"Directions to the Bar H," the blonde said with a knowing smile.

* * *

Gemma clenched the steering wheel as she followed Natalie's directions out of town. The tight grip did little to calm the nerves jumping in her belly. The last time she tried surprising a man in her life by showing up unannounced, things had ended badly. Not that she suspected even for an instant that she would walk in on Hank with another woman, but what if last night was a onetime thing?

Following a man to his home after a night of sex had a certain stalker vibe, and she was about to turn back when the GPS on her phone alerted her that her destination was approaching on the right. She braked harder than necessary, something that might have caused an accident in city traffic, but she hadn't seen a car for the last ten miles or so. A wrought-iron arch spanned a dirt road, a boldly scripted *H* with a prominent bar cutting through the letter at its center.

Far too curious to turn back now, she spun the wheel. Loose gravel pinged along the car's undercarriage, but Gemma barely noticed. She didn't know what she'd expected, but certainly not the sight of a rambling stone-and-log house nestled in the foothills of rolling mountains and meadows. An enormous red barn stood to the right of the house, along with a split-rail corral.

Despite Natalie's directions, despite her GPS, Gemma would have sworn she was in the wrong place until she spotted a familiar horse in the corral. She wouldn't claim to be any expert when it came to horseflesh, but she recognized the palomino. The unique jagged strike of white on Lightning's forehead was too distinctive to belong to another horse.

The closer she drove to the impressive house, the more confused she became. The driveway stretched out beyond the house to a multicar garage. The bay doors were open, and alongside Hank's somewhat-ancient pickup, Gemma spotted a brand-new model—the Rolls-Royce of trucks if ever she'd seen one.

Easing her rental to a stop, Gemma left the engine running. Maybe she'd misunderstood. Could it be that Hank *worked* on the Bar H? And if that were the case, then Gemma didn't want to get him in trouble with his boss by showing up and bothering him at work.

She had already shifted the car into Reverse, ready to back away, before Hank—or the owner of the Bar H— discovered her. Habit had her glancing over her shoulder, though what traffic she expected to find, Gemma didn't know. But the sight of Hank stepping out of the barn stopped her faster than antilock brakes. He wore a frayed straw cowboy hat, the rattiest pair of jeans she'd ever seen, and had clearly been hard at work…if the sheen of sweat on his naked chest was anything to go by.

He pushed his hat back on his forehead as he caught sight of her car. Surprise crossed his handsome face as he sauntered—there really was no other word for it—over to her car. A puzzled frown pulled at his eyebrows as she lowered the driver's-side window, letting in the scent of hay and horses and sun-warmed male. "Gem? Everything okay?"

He braced a hand on the roof of the car, bending slightly to look inside, and she suddenly forgot how to swallow. Or speak. Or breathe.

"I, uh…" Shaking her head, she forced herself to snap out of the sensual daze. "I am so sorry. The last thing I want is to get you into trouble."

His chuckle set off Fourth of July sparklers in her stomach. "Not sure what kind of trouble you could get me into, but it might be interesting to try."

"Janie told me you were a rancher on the Bar H, but this can't be your place, can it?"

"Last I checked. You want a tour?"

"Do I want...?" Still stunned, Gemma cut the engine as Hank opened the door. "Janie wasn't exaggerating, was she? About the acres and horses and cows?"

"Cattle," he corrected, "and no. Janie knows almost as much about the Bar H as I do."

Feeling foolish, Gemma allowed him to help her from the car. She stared, slack jawed, as she looked around at the gorgeous house and the rolling green hills that stretched out in all directions. At the corrals and barn and other buildings in the distance. "She said you hadn't been able to take time off in years."

"Well, that's true, but I guess that's more just because... there's nowhere I want to go."

"And that you work from morning until night!"

"Ranching's hard work. Being successful doesn't make the work any easier."

"And your truck—"

At that, his eyes wrinkled up at the corners. "My dad and I fixed that old thing up decades ago. It's a classic."

"You must think I'm such an idiot," she muttered. "Volunteering to help you set some money aside—"

"Hey." He caught her hips in his wide hands, pulling her body into the cradle of his. "I think you are amazing to have made such a kind and generous offer. But like I told you, I'm good."

"Still don't need me for my mind, huh?" Gemma tried to keep her expression teasing, but something of waking up alone that morning must have shown through.

Hank stared down at her, a mix of regret and uncertainty shining through as his gaze roved over her face. "I'm sorry about leaving the way I did," he said, "but my men were already expecting me back yesterday."

"Is that the only reason you left?" Gemma asked.

"I—I guess I wasn't sure what you expected after a night like that."

"I don't know what I expected, considering I've never had a night like that before," she confessed. Nerves clenched her stomach as she worried about blurting out too much, too soon. Trying to cover, she added, "But breakfast would have been nice."

"Okay," he said with a slightly relieved-sounding laugh that turned suddenly husky as he promised, "Tomorrow morning, breakfast it is."

"Don't get ahead of yourself, cowboy," she said, a giddy happiness filling her. "After all, there's still tonight."

Early morning sunlight streamed into the room. Not wanting to open her eyes, Gemma buried her face in the pillow. She reached blindly for the blankets, and her hand came into contact with muscle covered by warm denim. Her eyes opened instantly. She realized she wasn't in her own bed in the honeymoon suite by the first blink. By the second she remembered where she was and every minute of the night before…with Hank.

"Morning."

He was seated on the side of the bed, dressed only in a pair of well-worn jeans, and Gemma soaked in the sight of him as she rose up on an elbow. Realizing somewhat belatedly that he was doing the same, she reached for the covers but they were wrapped around her waist. Fighting the urge to cover her breasts and pretending like she wasn't blushing, she replied, "Good morning."

He brushed her hair back from her forehead and tilted her head up for a long, arousing kiss. Gemma forgot all about wanting to cover her naked breasts. She forgot everything but the memory of his body moving over her, filling her, and she ran her hand down his chest.

Hank caught her hand before it wandered too far and shot her a warning scowl. "None of that this morning. I've got work to do, but..." His words trailed off as he turned to the side and Gemma used the chance to tuck the sheet beneath her arms. "Not before I brought you this."

Gemma gasped as she saw the large metal tray and plates loaded with everything from bacon and eggs to toast and fresh fruit. "Breakfast in bed, as requested."

She laughed as he settled the tray with its mouth-watering offering on her lap and reached for the glass of orange juice. "And I didn't even say anything about the in-bed part."

"I aim to please."

"That you do," Gemma murmured before taking a sip of the tart citrus. She was more than pleased with Hank. She was head over heels in love with the man.

"And as much as I would love to join you, I have to go." He gave her a quick kiss and finished pulling on a shirt and tucking it into his jeans. Just the sight of his hands on his belt buckle had Gemma melting inside. "There's more coffee in the kitchen, so make yourself at home."

Make yourself at home. Oh, how Gemma liked the sound of that!

Hank must have, too, as they had breakfast the morning after and the morning after that and the morning after that.

Gemma spent those days getting to see a small part of the Bar H and the cattle operation Hank ran. She couldn't help but be impressed, not by his success so much as the pride he took in running a first-class operation, the care he showed to the animals on the ranch, and the respect and admiration of his employees.

She'd been spending more time at the Bar H than at Maverick Manor, which made it easier to forget that she was still on vacation and that her time in Montana was quickly coming to an end. But as she stood in Hank's sunny kitchen, waiting for him to finish up some paperwork before they headed into town for pizza and wings, a notification bell sounded on her phone.

Pulling the cell from her purse, she was startled to see an email from one of her coworkers. She'd worked at Carlston, Landry and Greer for almost ten years. How was it that less than two weeks away, her job—or was it her entire life in New York—felt as though it belonged to someone else?

For a split second, Gemma thought about leaving the email unread or deleting it entirely, but she couldn't bring herself to make that split-second swipe. Instead she opened the message and skimmed over the contents.

"Everything okay?"

She jumped at the sound of Hank's voice, spinning to face him as he walked into the kitchen. She shoved the phone into her purse. "Yeah, fine. It's nothing." The moment she spoke, a sickening lump formed in her throat.

How many times had she asked Chad that question? And how many times had he tucked his phone away and answered her with those same words? With that same lie?

And while she certainly wasn't cheating on Hank, she wasn't going to start lying to him either. "It was an email from someone at work. She's heard that the bosses have narrowed down their candidates for the promotion, and I'm on the short list."

Was her mind playing tricks or did his spine straighten at the mention of her job? She certainly wasn't imagining the distance between them as he stayed on the other side of the large island, with three feet of granite separating them.

He ducked his head, the brim of his cowboy hat shielding his face as he said, "That's great, Gemma. Now you'll have the chance to pick and choose the clients you want to work with, just like you'd hoped."

Would she? As much as Gemma wanted to believe her hard work had paid off, she couldn't help but wonder how much her stepfather's connections to billionaires like Wilson Montgomery had paved the way. And if so, then the expectation would be that she would bring in bigger clients with even larger portfolios.

"You know, you aren't the only one who hasn't had a vacation in years," Gemma said, her heart starting to pound even as she tried keeping her voice casual. The same way this whole relationship with Hank was supposed to be casual. But her heart was in too deep, and so quickly, she wasn't even sure when it happened. The night he arranged for the late-night picnic at Maverick Manor? When she'd kissed him after their horseback ride? From that first moment when she'd seen him rising from the pool?

It didn't matter when it had happened. Only that it had. And now what? She was supposed to get on a plane and leave Rust Creek Falls and Hank behind?

"I'm sure I could talk my boss into letting me have a few more days off."

Even as she said the words, Gemma fought the urge to cry. A few more days? Was that really all she was hoping for when a lifetime with Hank would never be enough?

"Gem..." His voice was deep, rough, not casual in the least as he rubbed his hand over the back of his neck. "A few more days..."

He shook his head, and faint threads of hope wrapped

around her broken heart, mending the shattered pieces. So it wasn't just her? He felt it, too? He wanted more, too?

"A few days won't make a difference."

Won't make a difference? Won't make a difference to whom? Clearly not to Hank, but to Gemma, those days would make all the difference in the world—especially if they would be the last few days she would spend with the man she loved.

And Gemma knew then that the days weren't the problem. She was. *She* hadn't made enough of a difference in Hank's life for him to ask her to stay. He was, in his nice-guy Hank Harlow way, telling her to go.

"You've got a promotion waiting for you. Hell, you've got all of New York City waiting for you. Rust Creek Falls can't compare to the life you have in the city. You deserve so much more."

So he was telling her to go for her own good. Which was exactly how her mother had phrased things when she'd sent Gemma away to boarding school. She and Gregory were only thinking of Gemma's future and what would be best for her. It was the same line Diane had used to explain why she had lied about Gemma's father. All for her own good. But if this was all for Gemma's good, why was she the one feeling so bad?

"You're right, of course," she said woodenly. "I should go. In fact, it would probably be best if I left now. I can get a good night's sleep at Maverick Manor before I check out in the morning."

"Gemma—"

"It's a long flight, after all. Back to New York." She kept talking as she backed out of the kitchen, as if the words were somehow propelling her feet to move. "Back to my real life."

Did he really not know how he had changed everything? Maybe she was still a city girl, but thanks to Hank, she now had the heart of a cowgirl—one who was so completely in love with a cowboy…who didn't love her back.

"Goodbye, Hank." The farewell grated against her throat, like old, rough wood leaving painful splinters of emotion behind. "It's certainly been a honeymoon to remember."

Gemma thought she heard him call after her, but she didn't slow down and she didn't stop. What would be the point of listening to what he had to say when he'd made it clear he wasn't going to ask the only question she wanted to hear?

He wasn't going to ask her to stay.

Standing in the foyer of Anne and Daniel's house, Hank waited while Janie gave her mom a hug, an overnight bag slung over one slender shoulder. He rubbed at the ache in his forehead, a pounding that hadn't stopped since Gemma had walked out. But that was still better than the ache in his chest where he feared his heart may never start beating again.

"You got everything, kiddo?" he asked even though he knew she pretty much had anything she might need already at the Bar H.

"Yep! All set."

"Janie, why don't you go wait for Hank in the truck?" Anne suggested. "I need to talk to him for a minute."

Janie sighed. "Are you guys gonna talk about me?"

Without taking her gaze off him, his ex-wife stated, "Not this time."

"Oh…" Her curious gaze moving between the two of them, Janie seemed to come to some conclusion. Giving a small scoff, she said, "Good!" and headed down the front walk.

"What's up, Anne?"

"I thought you might tell me. You look like you've been working yourself to death."

In the three weeks since Gemma had left, Hank had done little but work. Once, after losing his family's ranch, after losing Anne, the Bar H had been his refuge. Something that was truly his and his alone. Working the cattle, cutting the calves and riding the fences had been his salvation. Now it all felt like punishment.

"I'm fine."

"Fine isn't the same as happy. Your mother used to say that…about our marriage."

"Yeah, I know. But you and Dan *are* happy now, so everything worked out."

"Hmm. From what Janie's told me about your stay at Maverick Manor, you and Gemma were something more than 'fine' together."

Hank didn't want to think about Gemma or about how empty the house felt without her. How empty his heart felt without her. And he certainly didn't want to talk to his ex-wife about her! But he stopped short at the open doorway before turning back to face his ex-wife. "I owe you an apology."

Anne's pale brows rose. "What on earth would you have to be sorry for?"

"All those years, during our marriage, I didn't get it. I didn't understand why you couldn't…let go. Just get over Dan and move on." His hand tightened on the jamb as he confessed. "I get it now."

Too little, too late, but Hank finally understood. There were some things a woman—or a man—didn't simply get over.

"Oh, Hank."

Sympathy filled Anne's voice, the tremulous sound weakening the walls he'd retreated behind since Gemma had left, forming cracks and causing too much of the emotion he'd been holding back to start leaching out until his whole body ached. "Don't, Annie," he said gruffly.

But of course she didn't listen. "Did you tell Gemma how you feel? Did you ask her to stay?"

He gave his head an almost imperceptible shake. "What would be the point?"

"The point? Oh, I don't know! Only that maybe she would have stayed and you wouldn't be all miserable and alone."

"Well, thanks for that." He turned to leave, but this time it was Anne who spoke.

"You have no one but yourself to blame for letting her walk out."

Hank turned back, anger cauterizing some of those leaky emotions and keeping them from spilling out all over the place. "My fault? You think this is my fault for not asking Gemma to stay? Give me a break, Anne!"

Understanding why his wife hadn't been able to let go of the real love of her life didn't make the pain of learning that lesson firsthand any easier to take. "In the weeks before we got married, if you had found out where Dan was living, would you have stayed if I'd asked? If I'd begged?"

"The situation isn't the same," Anne argued before hesitantly asking, "Is it?"

"Gemma was here on her honeymoon. By herself," he added when her jaw dropped. "She broke off her engagement only a few weeks before coming here."

"Did she tell you why?"

"She did." But her ex-fiancé's cheating was too personal for Hank to reveal to anyone else. "She says she's over him but…"

Anne crossed her arms over her chest. "You don't believe her," she accused as if he'd committed an affront to women worldwide.

"She was *engaged*, Anne. I met her the day after she should have taken a walk down the aisle."

"And you're scared."

"What? No!" How had Anne gotten *that* out of anything he'd just said?

"You're scared," she repeated. "You and I met not long after Danny left town and left me. You were looking for someone to start a new life with only to find out I was carrying some serious baggage."

"Janie was not baggage."

"You know what I mean. Even if I hadn't been pregnant, I was still in love with another man."

Hank's heart cramped at the thought. Not of Anne's loving Dan Stockton, but of Gemma's being on the rebound from her ex-fiancé. Her lying, cheating *loser* of an ex-fiancé. "It's not just her ex," Hank argued. "It's all of it. Her job, her life in the city. And not just any city. New York City."

Though he didn't like to admit it, he'd pushed Anne into marriage all those years ago. Ten years her senior, he'd been older and he thought wiser. So sure that as long as he treated Anne with love and respect, she'd eventually come to love him in return. But even as a teenager, Anne had known far more about the gut-wrenching depth of true love. Where letting go was like losing the most vital piece of yourself.

He knew now because that was how he had felt watching Gemma walk away.

But he didn't want to push this time. Not when Gemma

might go back home, take one look around the bright lights and big city and realize all she'd been missing. Rust Creek Falls and their time together might soon be nothing more than a faint memory.

Shaking his head, he said, "It's for the best, Anne. Gemma's gone back to her life, and it's time for me to get on with mine."

Anne shook her head. "Keep telling yourself that, Hank," she warned, "and one of these days, you'll start believing it."

By the time he finished with the evening chores and took a quick shower, Hank's stomach was grumbling. The scent of pot roast his housekeeper had put in a slow cooker to warm filled the kitchen, and Janie had already set the table for dinner.

"Janie, time to eat!" he called out as he headed down the hallway toward her bedroom, but she didn't answer. Figuring she had her headphones on, Hank lifted a hand to knock on the door. But the sound of feminine laughter hit hard enough to freeze him in place.

Gemma.

Hank knew the two of them had been video chatting every few days since Gemma had left. He knew because Janie was always quick to tell him everything Gemma was up to back in New York City.

Gemma went to a new art gallery. Gemma saw so-and-so at a fancy restaurant owned by a celebrity chef he'd never heard of. Gemma had tickets to the theater. Gemma had forgotten all about him and the nights they'd spent together in the honeymoon suite and on the ranch.

Okay, Janie hadn't actually told him that last part. But with as busy as Gemma was, rushing from one exciting event to another, Hank couldn't imagine she was lying awake at night missing him…the way he was missing her.

Dropping his arm, Hank backed away from the door and headed for the kitchen, even though he'd lost his appetite.

Later that night after dinner and hearing all about Gemma's latest adventure—this time field box seats at the Yankees game, when Hank hadn't even known she liked baseball—he settled back on the couch. Janie was microwaving popcorn in the kitchen for their marathon movie night, watching some of her favorite flicks, when his cell phone on the end table beside him buzzed.

He glanced over, not intending to respond unless it was something urgent. He didn't know if it was an emergency or not, but Hank felt his heart stop as Gemma's name flashed across the screen.

He scrambled for the phone only to knock it off the table in his haste and send it clattering to the floor. He swore as he reached over the arm of the couch, his fingertips brushing the plastic case but unable to reach it. By the time he shoved the furniture out of the way, the ringing had stopped.

His heart pounding, he waited, phone in hand, to see if Gemma might leave a message. Instead only the words *missed call* appeared on the screen.

Hank didn't know how long he stood there, staring at the now silent phone. He could call her. After all, she had called him first. After three weeks of nothing, he doubted she was reaching out simply to tell him she'd caught a foul ball at Yankee Stadium. But before he could make up his mind, he practically jumped when the phone buzzed again—this time with an incoming text.

Not a foul ball, but she'd definitely thrown him a curve with the words that popped up on the screen.

Talk to Janie.

Hank would never consider himself fast when it came to typing on the tiny screen, but his thumbs were practically flying as he shot back a response.

Talk to Janie about what?

He was holding his breath, waiting for a response, but all he got back was more of the same.

Talk to her, Hank.

He didn't have time to ask what he was supposed to talk about before Janie came into the room, carrying a huge bowl of freshly popped popcorn.

"Ready, Dad?" she asked as she plopped down onto the couch, a few of the buttery kernels bouncing over the side. "Which movie do you wanna watch?"

"I was thinking we might talk first," he said, sliding the phone into the back pocket of his jeans before Janie could see the screen.

Janie wrinkled her nose. "'Bout what?" she asked before she shoved a handful of popcorn into her mouth.

Hank resisted the urge to take another look at the phone. Gemma hadn't bothered to fill him in on that part. "Oh, uh, I don't know. I guess just about whatever's going on with you."

She rolled her eyes. "It's summer break. Nothing's going on around here."

"So...nothing, huh?" Would it be too obvious to try to

text Gemma? Maybe if he went into the kitchen to grab some drinks…

Hank cut off the thought. He and Janie had had a relationship long before Gemma had arrived on the scene. He didn't need her—he didn't need anyone—running interference between him and the girl he would always consider his daughter!

But Gemma had been the one to make him face facts. Janie wasn't a little girl anymore—even if she would always be *his* little girl.

"No new kids at the community center?" Forcing a casual air, he asked, "Maybe a new boy?"

"Da-ad!"

"What? It was just a question." Clearly the wrong question, much to his relief.

After a moment of silence, Janie gave a shrug. "Kristen Roarke is putting on a play in town," she said, mentioning one of the Dalton siblings who had won several roles in a regional theater over in Kalispell.

"Well, that sounds like fun."

"Yeah," Janie sighed, sounding about as excited as he had at the idea of a new boy in her life. "It's a musical."

"Even better. You love to sing."

"Dad…"

"What?"

Leveling a look at him that made her seem so much older, she said, "You know I'm not any good."

"Hey! What do I always say it takes to be good at anything?"

"Hard work and practice," she echoed.

"That's right. So, how many practices have you had so far?"

"None. The practices come after auditions." Setting the bowl of popcorn on the wagon-wheel coffee table, she slumped back against the cushions, arms crossed over her chest. "But I'm not gonna try out."

"Janie!" Hank cut himself off before he could launch into a version of his dad's "I didn't raise a quitter" speech that had gotten Hank through the rigorous schedule of chores in the morning, a full day of school, and football practice in the afternoon and evening. His father's tough-as-rawhide approach had worked for him and for Hank, but for Janie...

Talk to her, Hank.

"Why don't you want to try out?"

"I told you. I'm no good. I'm not gonna get the part I want."

"So that's it? You're quitting without even trying? You're gonna..."

Let the woman you love walk away because you're too damn scared to ask her to stay?

Was that what he was teaching Janie? To walk away from what she really wanted? To give up without giving it her all?

"Gonna what, Dad?"

"The thing is, Janie, sometimes in life you have to take chances. You have to risk making a fool of yourself and falling flat on your face if that's what it takes to get you what you want."

"But, Dad, I don't want to fall on my face!"

"And you won't! I wasn't talking about you, kiddo. I was talking about me."

Janie snorted. "I don't think they'll let you try out for kids' theater."

"That's okay," Hank said. "I've got a bigger part in mind."

The role of a lifetime.

Chapter Eleven

Gemma jumped at the sudden blare of a taxi's horn. The people swarming the sidewalk around her didn't seem to notice the obnoxious blast, too busy talking on cell phones as they jostled for position and pushed toward the crosswalk. She'd been back in New York for three weeks, and everything still seemed so loud, so crowded, so overwhelming.

Every breath she took seemed coated with heavy black exhaust. How had she never noticed that before? Temperatures had hit ninety degrees already, the rising heat adding to rising tempers, and Gemma longed for the cool breeze and open spaces of Montana.

How could she possibly miss a place she'd called home for less than two weeks? Why did she feel as if the wide-open spaces were tied to her heart, calling her back and making her question why she had ever left? Could she really trade in the Big Apple for Big Sky country? And if she were honest with herself, did any of that longing have to do with the place she'd left behind? Or was it all tied to the man she'd left behind?

The man who hadn't asked her to stay.

She had wanted a Wild West vacation to remember. Falling for Hank Harlow had made everything about her time in Rust Creek Falls impossible to forget. Not that the friends she'd met there were making it any easier on her. Natalie had texted or emailed every few days with the latest gossip. Ellie Traub had gone through some old family photos and emailed Gemma the scanned images of her father. And Gemma and Janie had talked on the phone or over video a few times a week since she'd left Rust Creek Falls.

But even though Janie always made a point of telling Gemma her dad said hi, she had yet to speak to Hank. The one time Gemma had picked up the phone to call him, he'd let her call go straight through to voice mail. Only when she'd sent him the text about Janie had he bothered to respond.

Which had been another blow to Gemma's already bruised heart.

Still, she couldn't help wondering if he'd convinced Janie that she should audition for the play at the Rust Creek Falls community center. If anyone could help Janie overcome that fear, it would be Hank.

If not for him, Gemma never would have ridden a horse. Never would have learned to line dance. Never would have fallen so hopelessly, helplessly in love.

Even though each breath she took battered her bruised and broken heart, Gemma couldn't regret her time in Montana. Hank had done more than help her fill in a missing part of her past. He'd given her the courage to grab hold of her own future.

Her boss had been shocked when she'd given her notice, and he'd held out the promotion like a diamond-studded carrot in front of her. "You'd work with the top clients," he'd offered. "The largest portfolios."

Little had he realized, that promise was all the more reason for Gemma to leave.

It wouldn't be easy, but she was prepared to make sacrifices to live life on her own terms. Even if that meant selling off her wardrobe and moving out of her apartment. But while she would miss living in the city, that too would have its benefits. She had a feeling she could get used to working from home while barefoot and wearing a comfortable pair of jeans. Maybe she could find a pet-friendly building and look into adopting a rescue dog to keep her company.

Of course a dog would be happier with a fenced-in yard, where it could run and play. Or better yet, an area with no fences. Just miles and miles of green grass and towering mountains and crystal clear streams...

Gemma swallowed a laugh before it could turn into a sob. Maybe she'd just buy a ranch so her soon-to-be-rescued dog wouldn't miss out on a life she could only dream of. Only, it wasn't the ranch Gemma was missing. It was the rancher.

Rust Creek Falls can't compare to the life you have in the city.

What did he know about her life in New York anyway? Not nearly enough if he thought she'd be happier there without him than in Rust Creek Falls with him.

City girl.

That was what he'd called her from the start. He'd told her to go because he didn't believe she had it in her to stay.

Picking up her pace, Gemma stalked down the sidewalk, cutting her way through the pedestrian traffic. He thought he knew her so well. Ha!

If the last months had taught her anything, it was that she was done doing what everyone thought she should do. From now on she was doing what she wanted to do.

And she wanted to go back to Rust Creek Falls.

Gemma nearly stumbled at the thought.

Could she really do it? Could she really go back? Giving up her apartment and her designer wardrobe was one thing, but to leave the energy and excitement of New York for the rugged wilderness of Montana?

Sweetheart, I think you've got more grit and determination than any woman I've ever met.

As Hank's amused voice echoed through her thoughts, Gemma smiled for the first time since leaving the Bar H.

Hank Harlow, you have no idea.

Something inside her broke loose, and Gemma suddenly felt free, like she was riding on Lightning again, the green grass speeding by beneath her, the warm summer breeze blowing through her hair. She could almost imagine the rhythmic beat of the horse's hooves. Only instead of the dull thud of hitting rich Montana soil, she heard the metallic clink of horseshoes striking concrete.

Surely her imagination was playing tricks on her. Torturing her with memories. But as the sound grew louder, closer, the pace slowing from a trot to a walk, it was Gemma's heart that took off at a gallop, and she couldn't stand not knowing for one second longer.

It's a mounted policeman, she warned herself as she turned around. *Or a horse-drawn carriage from Central Park.*

It wouldn't be, couldn't be—

"Hank."

Her heart pounding in her chest, Gemma couldn't believe what she was seeing—a cowboy riding a chestnut horse down the crowded street. Not just any cowboy, but her Rust Creek Falls cowboy. The man who'd stolen her heart the moment he'd climbed up behind her on Lightning and given her the ride of her life.

Seeming oblivious to the pedestrians who'd stopped to stare, Hank swung down from the saddle, his boots hitting the New York City sidewalk. He looped the reins over a nearby parking meter as casually as if it were the hitching post in front of the Ace in the Hole.

She heard an older woman murmur something about John Wayne, and he tipped his hat at a couple of giggling teenage girls who'd pulled out their cell phones to capture the moment.

Gemma might have thought she was dreaming, but she'd never dreamed of Hank Harlow in his cowboy hat and jeans riding up to her apartment building. It was too crazy, too unbelievable, too perfect for her to have even imagined. Which could only mean one thing...

He was real, and he was here!

"Hank, what—what are you doing here?"

He turned back to the horse, and Gemma realized there was a brown paper bag hooked over the saddle horn. "You forgot this," he said as he pulled out her cowboy hat.

"Oh." Tears blurred her vision as she reached for the straw hat, but she could still see the wry smile on his lips.

"You always do get so emotional about clothes." But the amusement fled as the tears started to fall. "Ah, Gem, sweetheart. Don't cry." His hands were the rough, hard-working hands of a rancher, but his touch was whisper-soft as he brushed the tears from her cheeks.

"What are you doing here, Hank?"

"When I found that hat..." His throat moved as he swallowed. "I figured you left it behind because you didn't want it anymore. A Stetson like that doesn't really fit in in the big city."

"I love this hat." She'd been so upset that last day on the ranch when she'd barely been able to put one foot in front of the other, she'd forgotten all about it. And *she* didn't fit in in the big city. Not anymore.

But were they really standing on a street corner in New York, amid a crowd of curious bystanders, talking about hats? And then as she remembered why she'd been so upset that day, a burst of anger had her reaching out and slapping him in the chest with the straw brim. "And I love the stupid, stubborn cowboy who gave it to me and then told me to leave!"

He caught her wrist, pulling her closer into his arms. "I didn't tell you to leave. I told you to go home."

"I was home," she whispered around the ache in her throat. "With you on the Bar H."

He rubbed his thumb over the inside of her wrist, the simple touch enough to make her weak in the knees. "You needed to come back here."

His gaze searched hers as he plucked the hat from her hand and settled it gently on her head. "I needed you to come back here," he admitted, "to know that you were sure. To know that you wouldn't change your mind in a year or two or twenty."

"I love you, Hank, and that will never change. Not in a year or two or twenty."

Taking a moment, he looked around the busy street with the rushing traffic and towering buildings and at the crowd of strangers who'd gathered around them with a wry smile. "What do you think? Are you ready to give this all up to be a Montana cowgirl?"

"A cowgirl! I think I'll actually need to learn to ride

before I can call myself a cowgirl. So until I earn that title, this city girl will be a cowboy's bride."

Hank's eyebrows rose. "Did you just propose?"

For a panicked moment, Gemma thought she'd assumed too much. But then she saw the spark in his eyes, and she knew. "You're an old-fashioned guy, Hank, with an impressionable daughter. And I'm sure you don't expect me to give up my life here, move halfway across the country, just to shack up with you."

"That's true. But there are some things us country boys like to do ourselves."

Gemma gasped—a sound echoed by the female onlookers—as Hank knelt on the sidewalk in front of her. She blinked quickly to clear the tears blurring her vision, not wanting to miss a single detail of the moment she would cherish forever. The brim of his hat cast a shadow over his handsome face, but Gemma could still see the love shining out from eyes as brilliant as Montana's Big Sky. He pulled a small velvet box from his pocket and opened it to reveal a glittering platinum engagement ring.

"When I told you I was rusty, I wasn't just talking about my dating skills." Tapping on his chest, he said, "I was pretty sure this old thing had rusted shut, too. I never expected to fall in love. I never expected…you. You broke my heart wide open, Gemma Chapman, and I can't imagine my life without you in it. Will you marry me?"

"Yes, yes, yes!" Gemma couldn't stop saying the word as Hank surged to his feet and spun her around in dizzying circles until she tipped her head back in breathless laughter.

Amid the honking horns and squealing brakes, Gemma heard another sound—the whistles and cheers of the New Yorkers who'd stopped to witness and celebrate the sight of a real-life cowboy proposing on a crowded city sidewalk. Only as he set her back on her feet did Gemma finally say, "Just promise me that we aren't riding that horse all the way back to Montana!"

Hank glanced over to his borrowed ride as the horse tossed its head with a jingle of reins. "This guy's staying here while you and I have reservations for first-class plane tickets back home."

Home to Rust Creek Falls.

Gemma didn't know if she'd ever be a true cowgirl, but she could still be whoever she wanted to be. Wife, mother, lover.

"So, I guess the only thing we need to decide is where we'll spend our honeymoon."

Gemma laughed at the teasing glint in Hank's eyes. "At Maverick Manor, of course!" She couldn't think of a better place to start her new life with Hank than the hotel where her two-week honeymoon for one turned into a lifetime love for two!

* * * * *

COMING NEXT MONTH FROM

H HARLEQUIN

SPECIAL EDITION

Available June 18, 2019

#2701 HER FAVORITE MAVERICK
Montana Mavericks: Six Brides for Six Brothers • by Christine Rimmer
Logan Crawford might just be the perfect man. A girl would have to be a fool to turn him down. Or a coward. Sarah Turner thinks she might be both. But the single mom has no time for love. Logan, however, is determined to steal her heart!

#2702 A PROMISE FOR THE TWINS
The Wyoming Multiples • by Melissa Senate
Former soldier Nick Garroway is in Wedlock Creek to fulfill a promise made to a fallen soldier: check in on the woman the man had left pregnant with twins. Brooke Timber is in need of a nanny, so what else can Nick do but fill in? She's also planning his father's wedding, and all the family togetherness soon has Brooke and Nick rethinking if this promise is still temporary.

#2703 THE FAMILY HE DIDN'T EXPECT
The Stone Gap Inn • by Shirley Jump
Dylan Millwright's bittersweet homecoming gets a whole lot sweeter when he meets Abby Cooper. But this mother of two is all about "the ties that bind," and Dylan isn't looking for strings to keep him down. But do this bachelor's wandering ways conceal the secretly yearning heart of a family man?

#2704 THE DATING ARRANGEMENT
Something True • by Kerri Carpenter
Is the bride who fell on top of bar owner Jack Wright a sign from above? But event planner Emerson Dewitt isn't actually a bride—much to her mother's perpetual disappointment. Until Jack proposes an arrangement. He'll pose as Emerson's boyfriend in exchange for her help relaunching his business. It's a perfect partnership. Until all that fake dating turns into very real feelings...

#2705 A FATHER FOR HER CHILD
Sutter Creek, Montana • by Laurel Greer
Widow Cadence Grigg is slowly putting her life back together—and raising her infant son. By her side is her late husband's best friend, Zach Cardenas, who can't help his burgeoning feelings for Cadie and her baby boy. Though determined not to fall in love again, Cadie might find that Cupid has other plans for her happily-ever-after...

#2706 MORE THAN ONE NIGHT
Wildfire Ridge • by Heatherly Bell
A one-night stand so incredible, Jill Davis can't forget. Memories so delectable, they sustained Sam Hawker through his final tour. Three years later, Jill is unexpectedly face-to-face with her legendary marine lover. And it's clear their chemistry is like gas and a match. Except Sam is her newest employee. That means hands off, sister! Except maybe...just this once? Ooh-rah!

YOU CAN FIND MORE INFORMATION ON UPCOMING HARLEQUIN® TITLES, FREE EXCERPTS AND MORE AT WWW.HARLEQUIN.COM.

HSECNM0619

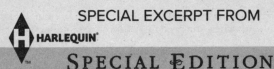
If the Satler triplets were a definite, adding this client for July
would mean she could take off the first couple weeks of August,
which were always slow for Dream Weddings, and just be with
her twins.

Which would mean needing Nick Garroway as her nanny—
manny—until her regular nanny returned. Leanna could take some
time off herself and start mid-August. Win-win for everyone.

A temporary manny. A necessary temporary manny.

"Well, I've consulted with myself," Brooke said as she put
the phone on the table. "The job is yours. I'll only need help until
August 1. Then I'll take some time off, and Leanna, my regular
nanny, will be ready to come back to work for me."

He nodded. "Sounds good. Oh—and I know your ad called
for hours of nine to one during the week, but I'll make you a
deal. I'll be your around-the-clock nanny, as needed—for room
and board."

She swallowed. "You mean live here?"

"Temporarily. I'd rather not stay with my family. Besides, this way, you can work when you need to, not be boxed into someone else's hours."

Even a part-time nanny was very expensive—more than she could afford—but Brooke had always been grateful that necessity would make her limit her work so that she could spend real time with her babies. Now she'd have as-needed care for the twins without spending a penny.

Once again, she wondered where Nick Garroway had come from. He was like a miracle—and everything Brooke needed right now.

"I think I'm getting the better deal," she said. "But my grandmother always said not to look a gift horse in the mouth." Especially when that gift horse was clearly a workhorse.

"Good. You get what you need and I make good on that promise. Works for both of us."

She glanced at him. He might be gorgeous and sexy, and too capable with a diaper and a stack of dirty dishes, but he wasn't her fantasy in the flesh. He was here because he'd promised her babies' father he'd make sure she and the twins were all right. She had to stop thinking of him as a man—somehow, despite how attracted she was to him on a few different levels. He was her nanny, her *manny*.

But what was sexier than a man saying, "Take a break, I'll handle it. Take that call, I've got the kids. Go rest, I'll load the dishwasher and fold the laundry"?

Nothing was sexier. Which meant Brooke would have to be on guard 24/7.

Because her brain had caught up with her—the hot manny was moving into her house."

Don't miss
A Promise for the Twins *by Melissa Senate,*
available July 2019 wherever
Harlequin® *Special Edition books and ebooks are sold.*

www.Harlequin.com

 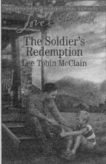

Looking for inspiration in tales
of hope, faith and heartfelt romance?

Check out **Love Inspired**® and
Love Inspired® **Suspense** books!

New books available every month!

CONNECT WITH US AT:

Facebook.com/groups/HarlequinConnection

Facebook.com/HarlequinBooks

Twitter.com/HarlequinBooks

Instagram.com/HarlequinBooks

Pinterest.com/HarlequinBooks

ReaderService.com

Love Inspired®

LIGENRE2018R2

Love Harlequin romance?

DISCOVER.

Be the first to find out about promotions, news and exclusive content!

Facebook.com/HarlequinBooks

Twitter.com/HarlequinBooks

Instagram.com/HarlequinBooks

Pinterest.com/HarlequinBooks

ReaderService.com

EXPLORE.

Sign up for the Harlequin e-newsletter and download a free book from any series at **TryHarlequin.com.**

CONNECT.

Join our Harlequin community to share your thoughts and connect with other romance readers!
Facebook.com/groups/HarlequinConnection

HARLEQUIN®

**ROMANCE WHEN
YOU NEED IT**

HSOCIAL2018

Reward the book lover in you!

Earn points on your purchase of new Harlequin books from participating retailers.

Turn your points into **FREE BOOKS** of your choice!

Join for FREE today at
www.HarlequinMyRewards.com.

Harlequin My Rewards is a free program (no fees) without any commitments or obligations.